APPLE CIDER ASSAULT
FIREFLY JUNCTION COZY MYSTERY
BOOK NINETEEN

LONDON LOVETT

Apple Cider Assault

Copyright © 2024 by London Lovett

All rights reserved.

No part of this book may be reproduced in any form or by any electronic or mechanical means, including information storage and retrieval systems, without written permission from the author, except for the use of brief quotations in a book review.

ISBN: 9798335188067

Imprint: Independently published

CHAPTER 1

"Magnificent, just magnificent," Edward said.

"Look! Look. Did you see that?" Jackson said excitedly as if he was a little kid watching a parade. "Look at the way he arches his neck when he picks up the lope. That's what we people in this century call *attitude*. That gelding has attitude."

"I agree. But one small point of interest—that's a canter, not a lope."

"You call it what you want. I think we can both pat ourselves on the back for this one."

I half expected Jackson to reach up and pat Edward on the back, only that would be futile since Edward was only the vaporous image of a man who lived two centuries ago at my home, the Cider Ridge Inn. Still, watching Edward Beckett stand next to his most recent descendant and my boyfriend, Brady Jackson, it was hard to believe Edward was no longer among the living. The men had finally found something that held both their interests—horses. Jackson built a fantastic barn in the pastures behind the house, and now we'd added a beautiful bay gelding named Cash to our farm. Coco and Sassy, our two goats, joined us last year, and they'd been an absolute delight, but the horse had the men positively swooning. The horse was, as Edward crooned, *magnificent*. His coat was a dark cocoa brown, which contrasted perfectly with a long black mane, tail and charcoal black socks.

Jackson laughed. "Did you see that little shake of his head? Total attitude."

Redford and Newman, my border collies, barked excitedly at the front door. I left the drawing room window and my secret viewing spot to answer the door. I was expecting Raine for breakfast. I had the day off from the office, not out of the goodness of the newspaper owner's heart but because Prudence Mortimer knew I'd be giving up my Saturday to cover the season opener at the local cider mill.

Redford and Newman kept up the clamor and enthusiastically urged me toward the front door. They knew Raine would have a pocketful of treats. Raine, my best friend and the town psychic, was the only person, other than Jackson, who knew about my resident ghost. She had more than a small crush on my nineteenth century inhabitant. It was hard to blame her. Edward was no longer flesh and blood, but he was quite the picture in his waistcoat and tall black boots. The posh English accent didn't hurt either.

I swung open the door. It might have been the swirl of fiery colors outside, but I could have sworn I smelled pumpkin spice in the breeze. "I've been knocking like an impatient trick-or-treater waiting for candy." Raine swept inside, her colorful skirt flowing around her legs. Redford and Newman sat down and waited for their treat.

I laughed. "Five seconds ago, they were barking and jumping around like two wild puppies, now they look like students at a strict prep school. How do you get them to do that?"

"My sixth sense gives me a little nudge in the animal world, too. Plus, they know they need to sit before they get their treat. What took you so long to come to the door?" She started off toward the kitchen, a logical choice considering the invite to breakfast, but I nodded toward the drawing room.

"Coffee is ready, but there's something you have to see first. It's the cutest thing since that viral video of the porcupine eating a pumpkin."

"I've seen your drawing room and yes, the throw pillows with the sheep are very cute. I don't have any coffee yet," she complained.

I'd left the window in the drawing room open. I turned back to Raine and put a finger to my lips to shush her. Her forehead furrowed in confusion and irritation because I'd pulled her away from the coffee aroma.

"I think he needs a good grooming," Edward said. "That coat will shine up nicely." Edward chuckled. "He'll be ready to stand for a portrait. I had my first portrait painted on my horse, Jasper. He was, in all honesty, a pony, but my seven-year-old self thought he was the finest horse in the county."

"I agree the last owners were lax on grooming. Although that winter coat is starting to sprout, so there won't be much shine."

"True. He does look woolly."

Raine and I hovered silently near the window. She covered her mouth to stifle a snicker. Until we started building the barn, Edward had never ventured out the back of the house. His world had been limited to the interior of the house and the front stoop. His keen interest and insistence on being included in the construction of the barn had caused him to step out of the rear of the house. It turned out the barrier to his world extended about ten feet out from the back of the house. It was the same distance he could move out on the stoop, so it made sense. He'd inadvertently added more space to his limited world, and he was taking full advantage of it. The horse added another layer to his existence, too. He'd been a skilled and devoted equestrian in his day, and he'd taken his task of finding Jackson a suitable horse very seriously. It had been fun to watch the process. I was amazed at how much Edward could tell based on photos and videos. In the end, they'd both agreed that Cash was the best choice.

"He'll look dashing under a nice, tan leather English saddle," Edward said. "A slick one with shiny silver irons."

"I agree, only I ride western, so there'll be stirrups on my saddle," Jackson said.

Edward's image spun out of focus as he turned toward Jackson. They probably could have spotted Raine and me at the window, but they were too focused on the horse. "You can't possibly be planning to heave one of those hideous, unwieldy western saddles onto that horse!"

"I'm not going to prance around on one of those patches of leather you British call a saddle. I learned western. It's way more comfortable than an English saddle."

"I beg to differ."

"Have you ever ridden in a western saddle?" Jackson asked.

"I wouldn't be caught dead in one. Have you ever ridden in an English saddle?"

"Nope, and ditto."

"Ditto? What term is this?" Their voices grew louder and more aggravated. The cute show was over, and we were back to the usual annoying man-banter.

I motioned for Raine to follow me out of the room. She did so reluctantly. "But it was just getting good."

"Nah, I hear their contentious stuff all the time. But you should have seen them earlier. They were like two young parents cooing over their newborn. It was really sweet. I would have recorded it if Edward could actually show up on camera."

We reached the kitchen. Newman and Redford trotted in behind us and then went to the back door. They were both a little freaked out by the new four-legged visitor in the yard, but their curiosity kept them going in and out all day.

Raine poured us each a cup of coffee while I cut slabs of pumpkin bread. It was my sister Emily's recipe, of course, and I'd done a pretty darn good job with it, considering baking and cooking were down at about fifth on my list of skills.

I popped the slices into the microwave. Emily had sent a few tips along with the recipe, and the main one was to eat it warm out of the oven or zap it in the microwave. Heating the bread in the microwave sent a shot of nutmeg and cloves into the kitchen.

"Hmm, that smells even better than the coffee." Raine sat at the kitchen table.

I carried the pumpkin bread over and sat down. "How did the date go?"

"First of all, Tucker was an hour late." She tried to sound angry about it, but I sensed, from the grin she was trying to suppress, that the date went well. "His boss, Shawn Griswold, works him too hard. He brought me a box of chocolates to make up for being late."

"That works. I guess Tucker has been having to put in extra hours because this is opening weekend at the Griswolds' cider mill. I'm covering the event tomorrow."

Raine quickly swallowed the bite she'd been working on. "Oh good, we can go together. I told Tucker I'd be there. He's in charge of giving lectures about how the cider is made. A job he hates," she added. "He's a maintenance man, but there's also no one who knows the working of that old mill better than Tucker."

"I know the Griswolds in passing, but I've never really met them," I said. "What kind of people are they? Will my press pass get a warm welcome?"

"Oh, I'm sure it will. Lots of publicity for their mill. Tucker says that Amanda Griswold is very kind and respectful, but her husband is always grumpy. He only ever points out things Tucker does wrong. Never gives compliments, and Tucker works hard."

"That's a shame. Everyone likes to be appreciated for the work they do."

Jackson walked in. The dogs trotted in after him.

"How is the new boy?" Raine asked.

"He's simply magnificent," Edward answered for Jackson

as he appeared in the kitchen. "I made a good choice," Edward continued.

Jackson raised a dark brow. "*We* made a good choice. It was a joint effort, remember?"

Edward shrugged his broad, transparent shoulders. "If you say so."

Jackson rolled his eyes and fortunately found a new focus. "Is that Emily's pumpkin bread?"

"Emily's recipe but made by these loving hands." I lifted my hands and turned them back and forth.

The hungry longing in Jackson's eyes faded a little.

"Oh my gosh, you're disappointed," I said. "Well then, don't have any. More for Raine and me."

"No, of course I want some," he said quickly, trying to make up for his very big misstep.

Raine tamped down a smile.

"Stop grinning," I muttered to her. "Or I'll just eat the whole loaf myself."

Raine sat up and wiped away the smile. "You're right. Like you said—everyone likes to be appreciated for their work, and this pumpkin bread is stellar. Possibly even better than Emily's."

I looked over at her. "Now you're just being annoying."

"Sorry. So, are we on for the cider event? I hear they're selling apple cider donuts this year, and I'm looking forward to trying one."

I'd been sufficiently insulted about my baking, but a cider donut did sound delicious. "We can go together. But remember, I'll be working. I can't stand around all day and watch you flirt with your apple cider man."

CHAPTER 2

*J*ackson and I both had the day off, but he had plans to put up some crossties in the barn, and then there was work to be done on the tack room. I was just as glad to break away from tedious chores (chores he considered fun) to have lunch with my sisters at Emily's farm. I was lucky enough to live right between my two sisters. Lana owned the farmhouse, complete with event barn, on one side of Cider Ridge Inn, and Emily and her husband, Nick, owned the adorable and highly productive farm, complete with equally adorable animals and an impressive vegetable and herb patch, on the other side. Emily, my younger sister (and the pearl of the family in beauty and temperament) and Nick had planned to make a living selling organic produce and eggs and had done an admirable job of it, but one day, my sister started a recipe blog. Now she spent most of her time in her farm kitchen developing delicious goodies like this morning's pumpkin bread. It had grown into a very lucrative business.

Lana also had a thriving business as a party planner. There was a year-long waiting list for her services. I'd planned to open the inn as a bed and breakfast, only I put the brakes on the whole idea when I realized what a negative impact it would have on Edward's existence. And, if I was being honest, I loved my job as a journalist, even if it meant sometimes covering mundane things like the season opener at the cider mill.

It was a wonderful fall day, complete with a crisp, almost biting breeze and a few wispy clouds in an otherwise blue sky. Lana and I decided a walk to Emily's farm was a nice excuse to put on scarves, beanies and coats. It had been a particularly long, humid summer, so the fresh, cool temperatures were greatly appreciated. Lana was wearing a bright orange scarf and an orange beanie to match. She held out her arms as I trotted down the front steps to meet her.

"It's my pumpkin outfit," she said. "I saw it online and I thought, orange—that's going to be my mood color for fall."

I adjusted my own forest green scarf around my neck. I had it piled up nearly to my chin and had to push it down to talk. "I think it suits you." The cool air and energetic breeze coaxed us to move faster. We were on the lane to Emily's farm in no time.

"How is the horse?" Lana asked.

"I think I've been replaced. But seriously, I haven't seen Jackson this happy in a long time. That job of his is so hard—mentally, physically, all of the above."

"Then it's a good thing he has you. Just remind him that the horse isn't going to help him solve murders." Lana was referring to my own side "job"—the one where I solved local murders. Fortunately, the summer had been quiet, and I'd been able to hang up my sleuthing hat for a few months.

Delicious aromas wafted through Emily's kitchen window as we reached the farmyard. Her massive flock of chickens (a feathery group of the sweetest, noisiest busybodies anyone could meet) raced around the yard to see if we'd brought them some nice greens or a few handfuls of scratch.

Lana held up her hands. "Sorry, gals, just a couple of selfish moochers coming for their own treats."

We walked in the kitchen door and got an even better whiff of the aromas. I took a deep breath. "Sage and thyme?" I asked.

Emily looked up from her stove. Her silky white-blonde hair was piled on top of her head, and her cheeks were pink from the steam. "Very good." Emily dipped a ladle into her pot. "Potato soup. I've been trying to perfect my already-mostly-perfect potato soup recipe. You gals will be my food critics."

"I love it," Lana said.

Emily laughed. "You haven't tried it yet."

"I'm starved, so I can tell you in advance—I love it."

Lana and I sat at Emily's farm table. Buttery scones were piled on a plate in the center of the table. "Do we get to taste the scones? I love those, too, in case you need my opinion," Lana said.

Emily carried two steaming bowls of soup to the table. "Do you think I'd serve my big sisters a lunch that was mostly vegetables without offering a side dish of bread? Help yourself. They're my plain, all-butter scones."

"There's nothing plain about something that's all-butter." I plucked a large scone off the top of the pile.

Emily carried over her bowl of soup, took off her apron and sat down across from us. "Nick had to go to the farm store. When the cold weather creeps in, he likes to double up on straw in the stalls. Keeps the animals warmer."

"I better relay that tip to Jackson." I broke off a piece of scone. "Although, with the way he's been fawning over that horse, I might just find Cash curled up in one of the bedrooms."

"That's so cute," Emily said.

"They're both acting like new parents," I said, not thinking. I froze for a second wondering how I was going to back out of this one. I'd never told Lana or Emily about Edward. The fewer people who knew about my implausible secret, the better.

"Who are you talking about?" Lana asked.

I shook my head. "This food is so good it's made me dizzy. I mean we're both acting like new parents."

Lana looked at Emily and shrugged.

I needed to switch topics. It had been many months since I let something about my ghost slip in front of my sisters. I was blaming it on the buttery scone. "Lana, have you met Raine's new boyfriend, Tucker?"

"Tucker Carmichael? Sure, he's a nice guy. A little sloppy in the fashion department, but I like him. I actually met him a few years back when I was planning Shawn and Amanda Griswold's twentieth anniversary party. He works for them at the cider mill. They wanted to have tractor rides for the guests, and I had no tractor to offer, so Tucker borrowed one from a friend and drove it all the way over to my property. He was the one giving rides, too."

"I'm covering the season opener at the cider mill," I said.

Emily looked up from her soup. "That's fun. I was planning to stop over there tomorrow. I know Annie, the pie baker. We often swap baking tips. She's created an apple cider doughnut recipe that I want to see in action. She reduces the apple cider in a hot pan, so it's a concentrated cider syrup. I can't wait to see how it's all done."

"I'll go with you," Lana said. "I need to buy some cider for a party next week."

"Hmm, seems like we're all going to be there," I said. "Maybe we can meet up. By the way, how are the Griswolds? I've got to interview them."

"Well, she's a little dull. Always polite. He's the exact opposite. But the marriage seems happy enough. I think she enjoys running the cider mill with him. No kids. She told me they tried, but it never happened." Lana finally put down the scone and tried the soup. "Hmm, yep, I was right. I knew I loved it even before I tasted it."

CHAPTER 3

The sun was starting to dip low in the sky. A cluster of clouds promised a pastel pink sunset. The buckeyes and sugar maples were working diligently toward the fiery colors of fall. It was my favorite time of year. The days were short and cool and crisp, but the snow was still a few months off, and the humid heat of summer was a month back. Autumn was the one season that really knew how to behave. Aside from the occasionally blustery day, there was nothing to complain about when it came to fall.

I sat on the back stoop to watch Jackson ride the horse around the clearing he'd made adjacent to the pasture. Coco and Sassy, the two goats, had insisted on joining me. They were both taking turns climbing the steps and then jumping off in the sweet and clumsy way only goats could manage. The dogs were sitting in front of the barn where they could get a better view of their favorite person (Jackson, not me) riding on the strange new family member. I'd taken at least a dozen photos, deciding Brady Jackson on the back of a horse was something that needed to be captured for eternity. His thick hair flowed behind him much like the horse's mane, and Jackson's broad shoulders strained at the flannel shirt he'd pulled on for the ride. A small sigh ushered out before I could stop it.

Edward made his signature scoffing noise. It was a sound somewhere between scorn and a pearl-clutching gasp of disapproval. I liked to tell him he would have made a perfect dowager duchess sitting imperiously in a big chair in her drawing room criticizing everyone for bad table manners.

"What is it, dowager duchess?" I asked.

"I don't know which is more irritating—the sloppy way he's handling that horse, or the ridiculous sound you make every time he rides past."

"I don't think he's a sloppy rider at all. He looks like a hero riding into the sunset in a classic western. He just needs a hat. And that sound I make comes from the heart, a heart that thumps a little faster every time he rides past." Jackson had slowed to a trot. "Hey, Jax, it's settled. I'm buying you a black cowboy hat," I called to him.

"Uh, don't you mean a white cowboy hat?" he called back.

"Please, everyone knows the cool guys always wore black hats." Sassy settled in behind me and started nibbling on the edge of my scarf. "No, you don't, Miss Sassy. You already chewed off one of my shoelaces." I gave her a nudge, and she flew off the step to join her sister for some grazing.

"You're too far forward," Edward yelled. It seemed he could no longer just sit in the stands as a spectator. He needed to coach. "And, good lord, quiet your hands. I've seen a monkey ride on the back of a dog and look far more skilled."

Jackson turned to stare at him as he rode past. He leaned forward a little bit more and started moving his hands in an exaggerated motion. "That good, Gramps?"

"Oh, come on, this morning you two were best horsey buddies. I was hoping that positive energy would last," I said loudly.

"Then talk to the column of vapor standing next to you," Jackson said on his next pass.

I peered up at Edward. He was a dashing column of vapor at that. "Maybe give pointers in a less obnoxious manner. For example—'I always found that the horse moved better when I sat back.' Oh, and leave out the 'monkey riding a dog' comparison."

"Fine." Edward waited for Jackson to come around the corner. "I always found that a horse moved better when I wasn't yanking at his mouth as if he was a child's pull toy." Edward looked down at me. "Better?"

"You almost had it, but it all went south after the word *when*."

"It's because of that unsightly hunk of leather he calls a saddle. His position and hands and feet would be much better in a proper saddle."

"Edward, this is how he learned to ride." We both watched as Jackson rode past. The horse seemed to be having as good a time as the rider. "He looks so happy. Please, let him enjoy this. He has a difficult job, and he's been looking so forward to getting this horse." It was rare when I asked Edward for some cooperation. Mostly because it was usually a waste of breath and energy. But this time he seemed to be taking in my words and, at the very least, considering them. He didn't respond, which was a touch better than the acerbic response I expected.

We both watched in silence for a few minutes. Jackson slowed the horse to a walk to cool him down before taking him into the barn.

"Some of the best moments of my life were on the back of a horse," Edward said quietly. As excited as he'd been to help Jackson on this venture, I worried that it would drive him into one of his melancholy moods. A horse would remind him how much he's missing and how much he missed by dying far too young. His wild ways had gotten him into trouble his entire youth, and as a young man, he'd had his heart broken and immediately raced back to his rebellious ways. He ended up in a duel with the American cousin who was kind enough to take him in after his parents all but disowned him. That duel ended in his death right here at the Cider Ridge Inn. I'd tried for months to find out why Edward had found himself stuck at the inn, seemingly never able to move on to eternal peace. A lot of research led me to the explosive discovery that the man I loved, Brady Jackson, was his descendant. Jax's ancestors had all come from the same branch of a family tree that began with Edward's indiscretion with his cousin's young wife. I was sure uncovering what I considered to be a satisfying ending to his story would give Edward the peace he needed to move on, but here he was, still floating around the halls and sometimes standing on the back stoop of the Cider Ridge Inn. I was convinced more than ever that he remained stuck between worlds because of a broken heart, only it had nothing to do with Bonnie Ross, his cousin's wife. It was Kat Garfield, the woman he loved. Unfortunately, no amount of research could provide me with a fix for that. Edward would never be with Kat. It seemed he would be here at the inn forever. In truth, I couldn't imagine living here without him.

Jackson dismounted. He raked his thick hair back with his fingers. Even with the unhelpful comments from his audience, he wore a smile that nearly broke his face in two. I hopped up. The movement immediately alerted the goats that it was time to follow me. I walked toward Jackson. "Wait, I need to get a picture of the two of you together."

Jackson slung his arm over the horse's neck, and Cash responded by nudging against him with his muzzle. I took a few photos. "All right. And it's definitely going to be a black hat."

"Well done," Edward called.

Jackson's eyes rounded as he looked at me.

"Don't make a deal about it. Just go with it," I whispered.

"Thanks, Edward."

"Oh, I was actually referring to the horse, but yes, well done...you."

Jackson shook his head. "Sure, just go with it," he muttered as he walked the horse past me.

I shrugged. "Thought we were having a moment. Guess I should have known better. But for what it's worth," I called to his back, "I was oohing and aahing the whole time. Seriously, I haven't made sounds like that since I went to an NSYNC concert in my teens." I realized my teasing wasn't helping. I ran over to catch up to him. "Jackson, I'm really glad you found your horse."

He stopped and looked at me. "Me, too, Bluebird. Me, too."

CHAPTER 4

The morning had started early with an unexpected text from Prudence. She needed me to switch gears and cover the weekly Small Business Society meeting this afternoon. There had been some trouble brewing between the members and the board, and she thought it was a story more suited to my style. (She was right.) Lauren, my coworker, would cover the apple event. Since the meeting wasn't until late afternoon, I still had time to go to the event.

Raine had pulled on a red sweater for the day. She'd splashed on some makeup and even a touch of lipstick. I turned the Jeep down the long road that led to the Griswold's cider mill. It was a stretch of road much like the one that ran in front of my house. There were a handful of farms on the strip, and there was plenty of land between them. Most of the summer green had faded to brown, and the trees dotting the landscape were showing off their new yellows and oranges. The cider mill had been around since Edward's time. Back then, apples were ground under a stone mill, and a horse or donkey supplied the power. The Griswolds still had a few hand-turned presses for guests to make their own cider, but their main production was much more modernized.

Cars and trucks were already filling the cleared space in front of the mill. "Wow, there's already a good crowd," I said as I pulled into a parking spot.

"We better buy our donuts soon before they sell out," Raine said.

I smiled at her. "And that is why we are best friends."

I zipped up my coat and pulled a beanie down over my ears. The morning air still had a snap to it.

"I smell cinnamon and spice and everything nice," Raine said in a sing-song tone.

"It's making my mouth water."

The young woman selling tickets to the event was wearing a sweater with bright green and red apples printed on it. "Enjoy your day. The first demonstration starts in an hour," she said as we paid for our tickets.

We walked through an open gate that was decorated with red and green balloons. There were various spots set up for taking pictures. A woman was desperately trying to get three small children to smile for a photo while climbing around on a pyramid of straw bales. There was little cooperation because the straw bales were far too much fun.

Dried cornstalks tied up with red and green polka-dot ribbons stood tall and frilly around the border of the main yard. A table filled with caramel apples had gotten the attention of enough people that the line snaked around the yard.

The old hand-turned apple presses were set up under a red

striped canopy. The line to churn your own cider was considerably shorter than the one for the caramel apples. A small, portable stage had been set up at one side of the yard, and there were chairs lined in front of it. A shiny blue drum set filled a good half of the stage. Lauren was at the stage talking to three people wearing matching flannel shirts and cowboy hats. One of the men held a guitar and another held drumsticks.

"That pretty woman with the caramel-colored sweater and holding the tray of cider samples is Amanda Griswold," Raine explained. "Oh, there's the donut kiosk. The line isn't too bad. Let's go buy a donut, and then you can meet Tucker." She glanced around the crowded yard. "I see his truck." An old green truck was parked under a maple tree. Several rake and shovel handles jutted out over the tailgate. "I don't see him. He's probably in the cider mill getting ready to give the demonstration."

We reached the donut stand and got in line. It was moving fast because they were only handing out donuts. "How are things going at O.K. Corral?" Raine asked as we waited for our turn.

"Let's just say there is one too many sheriffs at the corral. You know Edward. He can't keep his mouth shut…well…ever. He was handing out unwanted pointers as Jackson rode the horse, but I assume he'll get bored of the whole thing soon."

Raine's face snapped my direction. "But he just got that horse."

"No, not Jackson. Jackson is over the moon with his new horse. I mean Edward. He'll tire of it all, eventually…I hope."

"It's got to be hard for poor Edward watching Jackson ride

APPLE CIDER ASSAULT

around on a horse. Edward was a skilled horseman back in his day. I'll bet he misses it."

"I think he misses horses and riding more than anything—even more than eating." We reached the front of the line. "Two donuts, please." I handed the girl my money. "My treat," I told Raine.

We walked away each holding a hot donut in a thin paper napkin. The donuts were a crisp golden brown, and they were coated in cinnamon sugar. We moaned with pleasure as we ate the donuts. "Now I wish I'd bought more." I licked the cinnamon sugar off my fingertip. "Emi said the baker, Annie, uses a cider reduction. I can taste it. Can you?"

"I can. It's very—how should I say—apple-y."

"Probably the best way to describe it," I added.

"Sunni, there you are!"

I spun around. Lauren was hurrying across the yard in a pair of sable gray boots. She was wearing a pink cashmere sweater and faded jeans. Lauren was young, mid-twenties, and about as pretty and fresh-faced as you might expect for someone in that age group. She was also Prudence's niece. At first, I worried that Prue had hired a young family member and that she'd get preferential treatment all while being entirely inexperienced for the job. But I'd misjudged Lauren entirely. She came with a large set of social media followers, all gained from her intriguing sense of photography and witty way with words. She rarely covered serious stories and much preferred stories like this, the season opener of a cider mill.

Lauren bit her lip. "I hope you aren't mad that my aunt gave me this assignment. I was supposed to be covering a high school fundraising event, but the parents were arguing about whether it should be a car wash or a bake sale, so it never even got put on the calendar." Lauren tended to be flighty, like a hummingbird. No sooner had she told me about the school fundraiser when she was waving wildly at someone behind me.

"Have you met Amanda Griswold?" Lauren waved again.

I turned around. Amanda was no longer holding the tray of cider samples. She had a perfect smile, straight white teeth and two dimples for embellishment. She was a statuesque, slender woman, and the way she walked reminded me of the slim models on a fashion runway. Her wavy, light brown hair was tied up in a red and green checked ribbon. "Amanda, come, you have to meet my fellow journalist, Sunni Taylor," Lauren said.

Amanda reached us. "Sunni Taylor, nice to meet you. I read your column every week."

"That's nice to hear."

She smiled at Raine. "Have you come to watch Tucker give his demonstration? He's always so nervous about it. Maybe if he sees you, it'll help his nerves."

"I hope so," Raine said. She held up her empty napkin. "The cider donuts were delicious."

"Yes, we finished them in seconds," I said.

"I'll let Annie know. She's been working on perfecting that recipe since Valentine's Day."

"Amanda, we're going to need more cups at the cider stand," a man yelled from across the yard. He was dressed neatly in slacks and a nice sweater. He was pushing a dolly of boxes toward the cider mill.

"Right away, dear," Amanda answered. "Well, you girls enjoy yourselves. Nice meeting you, Sunni." She walked away.

"I haven't introduced myself to Mr. Griswold yet," Lauren admitted. "He doesn't seem easy to talk to like Amanda. Where are you off to now?" she asked.

"Just wandering around," I said. "I'll let you get back to work."

Raine grabbed my elbow the second Lauren walked away. "There's Tucker over by his truck. Come, he's been dying to meet you."

Raine pulled me along toward the old truck. A man wearing baggy, faded jeans and work boots leaned into the cab and then straightened. Tucker was a big, burly man with thick, muscular arms and a slightly round belly. His short hair was tucked under a cap. His skin had that leathery, tanned look of someone who spent most of their time outside. His brown eyes smiled as he spotted us coming toward him.

"There she is, the light of my life," Tucker cooed as we neared. Raine giggled in an uncharacteristically girlish way.

"Tucker, I want you to meet Sunni Taylor." Raine waved her hand at me with a flourish.

"So, you're the famous Sunni Taylor. I liked that article you wrote about the local car dealer adding premiums onto their prices. We need more journalists like you."

"Thank you, and I'm glad you found the article interesting."

Tucker leaned over and kissed Raine on the cheek. "What are you two pretty ladies up to this morning?" His face turned grim, and his gaze landed on something behind us.

"Tucker, what are you doing standing around out here?" It was Shawn Griswold, and he was wearing an angry scowl. "The mill isn't ready, and there are people lining up for the demonstration. By the way, I thought I asked you to lock up the gate to the back pasture. I just had to yell at a few teens who decided to play a game of tag out there. It'd sure be nice to be able to count on you to do the simplest tasks."

Tucker remained amazingly calm, but his face took on the flush of embarrassment. No one wanted to be scolded by their boss and especially not in front of friends. "I'll get right on it."

Griswold didn't give us more than a cursory nod. It was a wonder anyone visited his mill at all with such a sour disposition.

Raine took hold of Tucker's hand. "We better let you get back to work."

Tucker nodded. The pink of shame hadn't left his face yet. "Nice meeting you, Sunni."

"Nice meeting you, too."

Raine and I walked away. "See, that Griswold is positively evil," Raine said. "Nothing Tucker does is ever good enough. Should I tell him to look for a new job?" Raine asked.

"I don't know if you want to step into anything like that, Raine. It's still too early in your relationship to make that kind of suggestion."

"I suppose you're right. I feel bad for him, and now my mood is ruined. Maybe we should buy another donut."

"I won't say no to that."

CHAPTER 5

Tucker looked visibly nervous as he stood in front of the sizable crowd that had filed into the mill for a demonstration on how cider was made. He'd brushed his hair down and pulled on a clean pair of jeans and a semi-pressed shirt. He rubbed his palms on his pants as he waited for everyone to settle down. It was odd that the Griswolds expected their maintenance man to do the demonstration.

Raine leaned her head closer to mine. "I'm not sure if my presence is helping or hurting."

"You can tell he'd rather be anywhere but here. It seems like they could have hired someone from the historical society to do this demonstration. It's not that complicated. You wash apples, pulverize them and drain off the liquid. At the very least, Amanda Griswold, with her stylish appearance and manners, should be doing it."

Tucker cleared his throat loudly. He reminded me of a brand-new teacher who'd been thrown in front of a class of ruffians. "If I can have your attention, we'll start at the old stone press." The bones of the old mill had been left intact. Faded, worn wood planks made up the walls, and weathered beams crisscrossed the rafters. A new roof and some aluminum siding on the exterior kept the space warm and dry. Early historical photos had been blown up and hung on the walls. One showed that the old mill originally had a dirt floor. Now, most of it was cement with strategically placed drains for easy cleaning. In the center of the barn was the new, modern equipment, but the focus of the demonstration was in the corner where the old stone mill and hand-cranked press had been left as they were a hundred years ago.

Two granite stone wheels, one flat with a deep groove and one perpendicular and attached to a spindle in the middle of the flat stone, took up most of the corner. A shallow trench had been worn in a circle around the stones. It was the indentation left behind by the animals used to turn the wheel.

The crowd, hyped up on cider and cinnamon-sugar donuts, finally quieted enough for Tucker to give his speech. "This is the stone mill that the original owners used to mash the apples to pulp. The operators would harness a donkey or small horse to the wooden crank, and the animal would walk around the wheel over and over again until the apples were sufficiently pulverized. Talk about a boring job," Tucker said with a little chortle. Raine laughed, otherwise his quip fell flat.

A few teens had pushed to the front, less out of interest and more to be pests. "Are you going to put some apples on there?" one kid asked. "Jeremy, here, said he'll be the donkey." The other teen made a rather impressive braying sound.

"This is a historic relic, and it's no longer used to pulverize apples," Tucker explained patiently. I noticed a tiny twitch in his cheek that seem to get stronger as he went.

The jammed-in crowd was making the place feel stuffy. Or maybe I was just feeling secondhand uneasiness for Tucker. Either way, I wasn't in the mood to hear more. "I need some air," I whispered to Raine. I moved back, closer to the open doors. I was sandwiched between the refreshing, cool air outside of the mill and the thick, apple-laden humidity on the inside.

The crowd had scooted closer to the historic press. This time Tucker allowed the teens and a couple interested spectators to give the handle a few turns. An angry tone outside the mill caught my attention. I'd heard him enough this morning to know it was Shawn Griswold. It seemed I'd only heard his angry tone, and I briefly wondered if he had a polite one. The argument outside sounded more intriguing than the cider discussion inside. Raine was fully engrossed, but I knew that had more to do with the person giving the tour.

I stepped outside into the fresh air and made my way around the mill closer to where Mr. Griswold was arguing with a man in overalls. A hand truck stacked with crates of apples sat between the men.

Griswold grabbed a green apple off the top, held it in his fist and waved it angrily in the man's face. The man taking the brunt of his anger was tall and thin. He was wearing a tan trucker's hat that had the words *Jonah's Produce* embroidered across the crown. His long, thin arms were folded defensively across his chest as he glowered at Griswold. Amanda hurried across the yard to where the men were standing. I thought she might be there to intervene. Instead, she stood next to her

LONDON LOVETT

husband and listened to the argument without any additional input. She did, however, look concerned.

"We've had to throw away more and more of your apples," Griswold continued. He was still clutching and waving the apple. "They're pure mush. I've warned you many times about bringing me low quality apples. But I'm through with this aggravation. We will be finding a new apple provider."

That comment shocked Amanda enough that her face snapped Shawn's way. She said something in a much quieter tone, so quiet I couldn't make out the words, but I was sure she was reminding him not to be so hasty.

"We'll find someone, don't worry," Griswold told his wife. She smiled weakly at the produce man and walked away.

"Fine. I'll take these back then." The man grabbed the handle on the hand truck.

Griswold reached out and grabbed it before it could be wheeled away. "No, I need these today. We're expecting big crowds all weekend."

The man, Jonah, I assumed, sneered smugly at Griswold. "So, they're good enough for your big event, is that it? No, you know what? I'm going to take them with me. I don't want you to have to suffer all that *aggravation*."

I was definitely Team Jonah in this argument. You don't insult someone's apples and then fire them all while insisting you need their apples. The way Griswold treated people, it was a wonder anyone ever worked for him.

Jonah snatched the dolly from Griswold's hand and started dragging it across the uneven ground to the parking area.

"Now wait a minute—" Griswold yelled. He was still shaking his apple-filled fist. "I paid for those apples." The man didn't seem to care that the unseemly quarrel had spilled out into his festivities. People were watching the scene with interest.

Jonah stopped and turned back to Griswold. I waited for him to dump the apple crates off and leave. Instead, he grinned at Griswold. "I'll refund your money." He turned back around and strolled off with his crates of apples. Griswold's face was as red as the apples. It was a shame he had such an unpleasant disposition. He was actually quite handsome if you ignored all the grimaces and glowers. Jonah was probably going to take a loss, but it seemed it was worth it to him to leave Griswold without apples on the busiest weekend of the year.

"I think my presence was making it worse," Raine said suddenly behind me. "Aside from that, I couldn't watch him squirm anymore. He seemed so unhappy. I think he should talk to the Griswolds and get off tour duty." Raine glanced around at the crowd of people sipping cider and nibbling donuts and pie. "Did I miss anything?"

I shrugged. "Only another moment of grumpiness from the owner of the mill." My phone beeped. I pulled it out. "Yay. It's from Emi. They're on their way, and they're bringing sandwiches."

Raine patted her stomach. "Thank goodness. That donut was good, but now I need something more substantial. Let's grab one of those picnic tables, so we can sit down to eat."

"Good idea." I glanced over at Mr. Griswold. His face was no longer red. He was on the phone, talking animatedly to someone. Another produce man would be my guess. It's hard to make cider without apples.

CHAPTER 6

Raine and I bought four cups of cider and snagged a picnic table as it was being vacated by a large group. Lana texted that they were circling the parking area waiting for a spot. In the meantime, Raine and I sipped cider and watched as the crowd flowed out of the mill.

"I guess he's done with the demonstration," Raine said. "Poor guy. I think he has to do two more today. There he is." Raine sat up straighter and splashed a bright smile. Her shiny bangles glittered in the sunlight as she waved at Tucker.

Tucker walked across the yard with slumped shoulders and his head hanging down. "I'll share my sandwich with him." Raine decided as he crossed over to the table.

"We've got some sandwiches on the way. Sunni's sister is a great cook. Everything she makes is delicious, and I'm prepared to share my sandwich with you."

"That's sweet, Raine, thank you." Tucker tossed his leg

over the bench and sat down with a plunk. It moved the whole table.

Tucker released a long sigh. It seemed to deflate his big chest like air leaving a balloon. "Did that go as badly as I thought?"

Raine patted his arm. "You were great. Everyone was very interested, and you know your stuff."

I nodded along in agreement. "It's not an easy topic to make intriguing, but you did a fine job."

A faint smile appeared. "That's kind of you both to say. It would have gone easier if I didn't have to contend with all those teens. They always join in just so they can disrupt and take selfies." Tucker lifted his head higher and peered around in periscope fashion, then he relaxed again.

"You have a right to a lunch break," I reminded him.

"Yeah, I know. But Griswold always manages to spot me when I'm on a break or talking to someone and then he spins it into a whole lecture about not working hard enough." As he said it, he turned his hands up to show his palms. They were covered in blisters.

Raine gasped and took hold of one of his wrists. "What happened?"

"Got these blisters raking up all the leaves around the yard this morning. Amanda was adamant that the yard be free of leaves before guests arrived. She's all smiles and politeness, but sometimes she's as bad as him. I got here at the crack of dawn to make sure the yard was leaf-free. Can you imagine? It's fall. Leaves are everywhere."

"It's part of the beauty of the season," I said. "Watching them flutter off the trees and then making a point of stepping on them to hear them crunch under your shoe. That's fall in a nutshell."

"That's what I think, too. Anyhow, they promised to hire a few extra hands to do the raking, but when I got here this morning, Amanda told me they couldn't find anyone. I know a lot of kids on my block who would have gladly come out to rake for a little pocket money. The Griswolds are just too cheap."

"Speaking of the Griswolds," Raine said grimly. "There's Shawn."

Tucker's posture instantly stiffened. He glanced warily over his shoulder, and the stiffness melted away. "No, it's all right. That's Riley, Shawn's twin brother."

I looked in the direction of Shawn's brother. His hair was longer and less neatly combed. His shirt was untucked and his faded jeans were torn at the knees. Other than the identical face, nothing about the man said "Shawn Griswold's twin." Riley also walked with a noticeable limp.

"Did he get hurt?" Raine asked. "He's limping."

"He was a soldier in Iraq. He got too near an explosive, so they had to rebuild the bottom half of his leg. Shawn and Riley inherited this cider mill from their parents, but Riley wanted nothing to do with it, so Shawn bought him out. He has a landscape business that does very well. I went to school with both of them and used to play soccer with Riley. You hear about twins being very close, but those two men couldn't be more different. They don't hang out together often." Riley spotted Tucker and smiled. He headed their direction. "And you'll soon see that Riley is much friendlier."

"Hey, Tuck." Riley and Tucker shook hands. Riley was far

more handsome than his disagreeable brother even though they shared the same face. Riley nodded and smiled at each of us. "Tucker, I guess I'm not surprised to see you sitting with beautiful women."

"Riley, this is my girlfriend, Raine, and this is her friend, Sunni."

Being called his girlfriend nearly lifted Raine right off her bottom. She smiled at Riley. "Nice to meet you."

"Much nicer than meeting my brother, I imagine," Riley teased.

Raine and I laughed.

Riley's gaze was pulled to someone behind us. "Oops, there's my grumpy brother now. He texted that he needed help, so dutiful sibling that I am, I drove straight over." He chuckled. "After I finished watching the soccer match on television, of course. Nice to meet you ladies." He limped off toward Shawn. Shawn had his fists on his hips as if he was already planning to lecture his brother for being late.

"He seems very different than his brother," I said. As I turned around, I realized that Tucker was ducking down trying to make himself small. Not an easy feat given his size.

"Sunni, here come your sisters," Raine said. "Have some lunch before you get back to work, Tucker. I promise it'll be delicious." Raine spoke fast to convince him, but Tucker was already getting up from the bench.

"No, I've got some snacks in the truck, and I don't want to get in the way of your lunch. Besides, I need to get the mill ready for the next demonstration." He took Raine's hand and kissed the back of it, then lumbered away quickly.

"Can you imagine working for someone like Shawn Griswold?" Raine said with a sad shake of her head. "Where you can't even relax enough to eat lunch. And Tucker told me he hasn't had a raise in over a year. He's planning to ask the Griswolds for one after this busy weekend."

"I'd say whatever they're paying him, it's not enough." I waved to catch Emily and Lana's attention.

"This place is crowded," Lana said in exasperation as if she'd just run a maze of obstacles.

Emily placed a canvas tote bag on the table. "Egg salad on fresh sourdough."

"That works." I reached inside the bag for a sandwich.

Emily looked at the cups of cider. "I see you bought some cider to go with lunch. What about the cider donuts?"

I was midbite when she asked the question. My eyes slid over to Raine. She was wearing a guilty grimace.

"Oops," I said before getting that long-awaited bite.

"Oh, very nice. We bring you lunch, and you couldn't be bothered to buy us donuts," Lana said.

"Emi's the one who made the lunch," I reminded Lana. "And I'm sorry, Emi. It was very selfish of Raine and me. But I will tell you they were delicious, and it's a shame you didn't get to taste them."

Emily sat down with a raised brow. It was always adorable watching my angel-faced sister try to look mad. "I'm going to see Annie after this. Hopefully, she'll have some extras."

Lana finished a bite of sandwich. "Wasn't that Tucker I saw leaving the table? You should have asked him to stay."

"He didn't want to interrupt our lunch," Raine explained. "Besides that, he spent the few minutes he was here chatting with us literally looking over his shoulder for his boss to come out from his usual cluster of dark shadows. That Mr. Griswold is the Grinch of the apple world."

Lana nodded as she finished another bite. "Yep, that's the Shawn Griswold I remember. Penny-pincher, too. You should tell Tucker to find a new job." Lana tossed that suggestion out casually.

"As I told Raine, it might be early in their relationship for that kind of suggestion," I said.

"I agree with Sunni." Emily put down her sandwich and picked up the cider. "He'll think you're trying to run his life."

Lana shrugged. "Nothing wrong with that."

We all looked at Lana with dismay.

She finally noticed after she lowered her cider cup. "What? I just think sometimes it's O.K. to take control."

I looked over at Emily. "And she insists she's not a control freak."

Lana picked up her sandwich. "What can I say? We first-borns—that's what we do. The world would be complete chaos without us."

CHAPTER 7

We lingered at the table a bit too long, considering there were people who needed a place to sit for lunch. Emily had added a bonus treat of her oatmeal cookies to the lunch tote, and they were a perfect ending for an autumn lunch.

"Lana, you're a member of the Small Business Society, aren't you?" The meeting, and the focus of my latest assignment, was less than two hours away.

Lana rolled her eyes. "SBS? Yes, big regret. Lots of dues and constant emails and confusing letters and very few benefits. They do step in, supposedly, whenever your business takes a financial hit due to unforeseen health or financial catastrophe. I've never had to use them for that…thankfully. Why do you ask?"

"I'm covering a meeting today. Prudence wants me there because she thinks it will get contentious and possibly controversial."

Lana was nodding along with that assessment. "Prudence Mortimer is a member, too. I've sort of lost interest in the whole thing because it's always like a soap opera in those meetings, but from what I've heard and read in a few of the unofficial Facebook groups, they're short on funds and haven't been able to help the few businesses that asked for assistance. It's kind of hard to believe because the dues aren't cheap, and very few businesses ask for help. I saw Tracy Goodwyn, the treasurer of SBS, wandering around with a cup of cider as Emily and I entered the yard."

"Oh, really?" I asked.

"Not too coincidental. Tracy is Shawn Griswold's cousin. She's a bank manager by trade and one of those women who wears impractical high heels and pencil skirts no matter what the occasion."

Emily laughed. "The woman with the bright blue heels and the skirt that didn't let her take a decent step? I thought she looked out of place out here."

"That's Tracy. She must have a thousand pairs of shoes. I swear I've never seen her wear the same pair twice. And they're always the high dollar ones, too."

Emily's tiny nose was wriggling as she lifted her chin. "Do you guys smell smoke?"

It took the rest of us a second to realize she was right. There was smoke in the air. Seconds later, a fire alarm shrieked.

"It's coming from the house," I said.

We weren't the only people to notice smoke, especially when a plume of it seeped out as the back door of the house opened. The Griswold's house was an early twentieth-century farmhouse that had been restored and brought back to its original beauty. It was painted white with dark green shutters and looked like the quintessential farmhouse. The woman who came stumbling and coughing out of the house looked to be in her fifties. Her light blonde hair was dappled with gray, and it was pushed back off her face with a green headband. She was wearing a checked apron that was dotted with flour. Her face was red from coughing.

"That's Annie," Emily said as she hurried ahead.

We caught up to Annie, while a few of the men, including Shawn, dashed into the house. Seconds later, windows were pushed open, and the smoke began dissipating.

"I only took a quick break," Annie started telling anyone who would listen. She spotted Emily's familiar face and grabbed her hand. "It was just burnt pies. There was no fire. But I only turned my attention away for a second. I hadn't had a break all morning."

Amanda caught up to us. She looked properly concerned. "Annie, my goodness, are you all right?"

"Amanda, I just took a little break. I hadn't had one all morning, and I needed to—well, the pies burned." Annie sobbed lightly.

Emily put a hand on Annie's shoulder. "It's just a few pies. The important thing is that you're all right." Emily looked to Amanda for agreement.

Amanda forced a smile. "Yes, that's what's important." She quickly switched her concerns. "How many pies were lost? We still need at least three dozen for the rest of the day and tomorrow." Amanda glanced toward the house. "It'll take hours for the kitchen to clear of smoke. I imagine the uncooked pies will be ruined as well." Her words were making Annie shrink down in sadness.

Then, to add insult to injury, Shawn Griswold joined us. "Please explain to me how something like this happened. You have a simple enough job baking treats to sell. How does someone let six apple pies burn? That is a state-of-the-art, commercial-grade kitchen. We've provided you with everything a baker needs."

"Except an assistant," I said curtly. "She wasn't given a break all morning. I'm sure that's not legal."

His face turned red. "And who are you?" he barked.

Amanda leaned over and whispered something into his ear. Some of the angry color in his face disappeared. "How many reporters did that nosy old woman send to cover this event?" Shawn asked.

"I was just here as a visitor, but I'll let the nosy old woman know how you feel about her reporters." I smiled. "I'm sure she'll want to hear all about it."

Shawn ignored my threat, but he was clearly flustered by my presence. Unfortunately, he turned his wrath toward his sobbing employee. "Since you are not capable of baking pies without burning down the whole house, you can consider this the end of your employment."

Both Annie and Amanda gasped.

"But we need pies for tomorrow," Amanda selfishly reminded her husband. They really did deserve each other. "Shawn, please reconsider."

Shawn shook his head. "My mind is made up. The kitchen is a mess, and the smoke has drifted into the rest of the house. We might have to hire experts to rid our belongings of the smell. That'll come out of your last paycheck." He turned sharply on his heels and marched away.

Annie was fully sobbing now. Amanda gave her an almost patronizing pat on the back. "I'm sure I can talk him out of this."

Annie sniffled and took a deep breath. "I wouldn't work for that man again if he was the last employer on earth." She struggled to untie her apron in the back. I circled around and helped her get the knot out. She was hoping to make a dramatic exit, but the apron had gotten in the way.

Frustrated, she yanked the apron off and handed it to Amanda. "Have fun baking your own pies." Amanda's pretty face drooped into a sour frown. "I'm going to get my things and leave this place for good," Annie added.

Emily asked if she needed help, but Annie wasn't in the mood to talk to anyone, even her friend, Emily. I couldn't blame her. She got a raw deal. Any more events like this and the Griswolds would have to run this place all by themselves.

CHAPTER 8

The smoke had all but cleared from the yard, leaving behind an earthy sweet smell that reminded me of cooking s'mores over a firepit.

As if he didn't have enough to do, Griswold ordered Tucker to carry some of the upholstered furniture out of the house to air out. He was still wearing the clean pants and shirt for the next demonstration as he hauled heavy pieces of furniture down the back steps. We tried to help by taking the pieces from him at the steps and placing them strategically around the yard where they weren't in the way of the activities. Fortunately, many of the visitors had had their share of apple treats and gone home for the day. The smoke incident had sent more people back to their cars as well. I was sure that would also be blamed on poor Annie. Emily tried to text her a few times, but there was no response. I told Emily she was going to need time to get over her rage and disappointment first.

It seemed most of the upholstered furniture from the first

floor was sitting out in the noonday sun by the time Tucker was called back for a cider demonstration. He looked, much like his name, tuckered.

"Well, I don't know about you gals, but I've had more than my share of apple activities today," Lana said. Emily was nodding in agreement.

"Yep, I've got to get to the Small Business Society meeting soon." My comment was mostly for Raine. It seemed she was more reluctant to leave. She was worried about Tucker.

"I hope he'll be all right," Raine said, ignoring our comments.

"He's a grown man," I reminded her. "And if he really feels mistreated, then I'm sure he'll start looking for a new job."

Raine's mouth pulled tight. There was something she wasn't telling us.

"Raine? What is it?"

She sighed. "I think he's worried he won't be able to find a new job. Griswold agreed to hire him even though he had a —" She paused and her cheeks blushed.

We all waited for her to continue. She'd left her sentence on quite the cliffhanger, so we weren't ready to back down.

"All right," Raine huffed. "Tucker was arrested for theft when he was in his twenties. He stole some tools out of his neighbor's garage. He was going to give them back after he fixed his car," she added. "But the neighbor was a crank, just like Griswold."

"Only Shawn Griswold was nice enough to hire a man with a record," Lana said.

"Yeah, I guess that's one way to look at it. He had a hard time getting anyone to even interview him, but the Griswolds needed a maintenance man, and Tucker is very handy with tools."

"Clearly," Lana said wryly.

"See, I knew I shouldn't have told you."

"It's all right, Raine," I said. "It happened a long time ago, and I guess it explains why Tucker is willing to put up with so much abuse from his boss."

"Speaking of that—" Lana muttered, "Mrs. Boss is heading this way."

Amanda was rubbing her hands together in worry as she walked toward us. I knew it was only because she needed pies baked. "Emily?" she asked tentatively, "you're Emily Cassidy, right? I recognize you from your blog. I knew you were local. I've been looking for a new source for eggs. I plan to start buying your eggs as soon as I run low." She was buttering up my sister, and we all knew what was coming next. "Annie talks about you all the time. She said she uses your recipe for her pie crusts, and they are so flaky and delicious—the best I've tasted."

"Why don't you cut to the chase," Lana said bluntly. My oldest sister had a low tolerance for superfluous flattery and beating around the bush. Our mom liked to say Lana came out of the womb knowing exactly what she wanted and how to get it.

"Emily, I'd be so grateful, and I'll pay you twenty-five dollars a pie. I'll give you all the ingredients. We'll need two dozen by tomorrow morning."

Emily was one of those people who hated to say no, especially when someone needed help. I just wasn't convinced the Griswolds were worthy of help.

"I can bake two dozen by tomorrow, but I want forty bucks a pie," Emily said in take-it-or-leave-it fashion. She wasn't feeling her usual charitable self either after the way her friend Annie had been treated. If I knew her, she was already planning to give the money to Annie.

Amanda bit her lip in thought then nodded. "Agreed. That just leaves me with the donuts. I watched Annie make them, so how hard could it be?" How hard could it be was usually a rhetorical question, but she looked at all of us hoping for an answer. Lana and I bowed out because we knew absolutely nothing about donuts except how to eat them.

"Donuts are tricky," Emily offered.

Amanda's brow arched with a new plan. "Maybe you could make some donuts, too?"

"I've never made them so no. I came here to learn the technique from Annie, but since you just let your brilliant baker walk away, I'm afraid you'll have to make the donuts yourself."

Amanda shrugged. "Maybe people won't notice if we don't offer the cider donuts."

"We all came here today specifically for those donuts," I said with a little too much enthusiasm.

Amanda's model posture slumped some. "Then I guess I'll have to give it a try. If you could please have the pies here by eight," she said almost dismissively before walking away.

"And that, my friends, is how *not* to treat people who agree to lend a helping hand," Lana said. "Maybe you should put a little too much salt in those crusts."

Emily looked at her, letting her know it was a ridiculous

suggestion. "Right, and then everyone will learn that I baked them, so it'll be my reputation ruined."

Lana shrugged. "Well, if you're going to get technical about it." Lana straightened. "Oh look—actually, don't look right now, because she's heading this way. It's Tracy Goodwyn, the treasurer of the SBS."

We'd been told not to look but decided to ignore Lana's request. I was curious to meet the woman since there seemed to be some financial issues within the society, and she, being the treasurer, would oversee finances. "Introduce me," I said to Lana.

Tracy Goodwyn looked to be in her early forties. Her short, brunette hair was stylishly swept over to a side part and her lips, bright with lipstick, were puckered as if she'd been sucking on a lemon. Watching her struggle across the uneven grass on high heels was a sight to behold. Her initial journey seemed to have been in our direction, but she paused for a moment to talk to Amanda. They were too far away for us to hear the exchange, but none of it looked particularly congenial, especially considering they were family.

"Those look like sharp words," Raine said. She was right. Tracy leaned forward to get her point across, a point that didn't seem to be about not getting a cider donut. Something much more grave was being discussed. And Amanda, who had started the day looking as if she belonged in a beauty contest, appeared more disheveled and less pulled together by the moment. She leaned forward, too, and even managed to point a finger at Tracy.

I glanced over at Raine. "Any chance that sixth sense can tell us what they're saying?"

Raine looked annoyed. "It allows me to predict the future and speak to people in the great beyond. I'm not a lip reader."

"Not unless they're ghost lips," Lana added.

I hadn't meant for this to turn mean, but when it came to Raine's talents, Lana was always too glad to put in her two cents. Fortunately, she also knew when she'd gone too far. "Sorry. I think I'm just grumpy because I didn't get one of those donuts."

Tracy and Amanda had finished their chilly conversation. Amanda walked away looking rigid with anger. Tracy would have, too, only she had to dedicate most of her posture and concentration to her walk across the grass in high heels.

"Why do women put themselves through such torture?" Raine asked.

Tracy put on a cheap, salesclerk kind of smile as she reached us. "Lana Taylor, I thought that was you." It wasn't surprising to find that the woman who wore spiky heels to a cider mill would be an air-kisser. My sister, on the other hand, not so much. There were an awkward few seconds when Tracy went in for the air kiss, and my sister reacted just as I expected. She leaned back out of range.

Tracy brushed it off with a light laugh. "I guess this event hasn't been going too well today. All kinds of snafus." There was plenty of glee in her tone, even if she tried to frown about her cousin's bad luck.

I cleared my throat to prompt Lana into action.

Lana straightened. "Ah, right. Tracy, these are my sisters, Emily and Sunni, and my friend, Raine. Sunni is a reporter for the *Junction Times*."

Tracy kept up the salesclerk grin. "Of course, I read your

column. Nice to finally meet you. Prudence Mortimer tells me you'll be at our SBS meeting today. I'm not sure what kind of story you'll get. It'll just be a regular housekeeping type meeting."

"I've heard there's been some questions and complaints about where our dues are going," Lana said.

Tracy wouldn't allow my sister to fluster her, even though she was giving it the good ole college try.

"Those are only rumors put out by disgruntled business owners. They start up businesses and can't turn a profit, then they come to us to bail them out. Anyway, come if you like. There won't be much to see."

It sounded like a not-so-casual attempt to keep me out of the meeting, so I was now more intrigued by my assignment.

"Well, I need to get over to the office. Nice meeting everyone." She strolled away, only it was a slow exit because her heels kept jamming into the soft ground.

We all watched as she made her painstaking way across the rest of the yard. "We're going to have to get out there, like they do at a polo match, and tamp down all the divots," I said. "Well, I should head over to that meeting, too."

"We can drive Raine home," Lana said. She was making up for the earlier comment.

"Thanks. Suddenly, that dull 'housekeeping' meeting sounds like it's going to be a great story."

CHAPTER 9

The Small Business Society held its meeting in one of the spare rooms in the city council building. It was one of those sparsely decorated, afterthought rooms where someone had pinned a few posters about safety and public events to a gray wall. A long table, like the kind used in the school library, sat in front of a retractable screen. Three chairs were lined up at the table on each side of the screen. Folding chairs were set in rows across from the table and on either side of a projector cart. It looked like the world's saddest lecture hall. All it was lacking were those funny little side-table desks they made us squeeze into for college classes.

I was the first person in the room. The smell of coffee drifted ahead of a small man with wire-framed glasses and a slight shoulder hunch. The cart he was rolling had a large silver coffeepot, stack of Styrofoam cups, packets of dried creamer and a plate of store-bought sandwich cookies. Dues were definitely not going toward making their meetings more inviting.

Since I wasn't a member, I took a seat at the back corner. That way, if things were as dull as Tracy predicted, I could cut out early without disrupting the meeting. It also gave me a good vantage point to watch the action if things did get heated. I was an outside observer who had no stakes in this meeting except to get a story. Prudence wasn't the type to start rumors, so I could only assume she knew something more than housekeeping was on the agenda.

The man placed the cart at the back of the room and then peered at me over his glasses. "Are you in the right room? This has been reserved for the Small Business Society meeting."

My press pass was still under my coat. I pulled it free. "Sunni Taylor with the *Junction Times*. I'm here to cover the meeting this afternoon."

He didn't seem to know how to react to my news. "What on earth for?" he finally stuttered out.

"Just a local interest story. My boss, Prudence Mortimer, sent me."

"Mrs. Mortimer?" His glasses slid down his nose, and he pushed them back up.

I had to admit it was always fun to drop Prudence's name into any chat. I usually got a range of reactions—anything from petrified, as if I'd dropped the name "Voldemort" into the conversation, to starry-eyed, as if I'd namedropped Queen Elizabeth. This man was somewhere in between.

"Well, help yourself to the coffee," he sputtered once he'd found his tongue. He hurried out of the room. I settled into my seat, and a few minutes later, a group of people walked in.

They all glanced my direction but apparently just assumed I was in the wrong room. The group, three men and four women, sat close to the front. Once in their seats, they huddled together and murmured in hushed tones. They kept a close eye on the door, too. All of them straightened in their chairs when high heels clicked on the hallway tile floor. A few more people trickled in, and then the high heels reached the room.

Tracy had on a new pair of orange heels and a straight skirt and coat to match. Her eyes flitted to me first because I was sitting alone, like an island, in a sea of empty chairs. I was sure I detected the slightest eyeroll, but she didn't have time to focus on the pesky reporter. The group up front seemed to raise her hackles. She tugged importantly on the hem of her coat, shook off something that I would label as irritation and marched to the front table.

The man with the coffee shuffled in next. His shoulders hunched more when he spotted the group sitting up front. More people trickled in for a few minutes. People chatted and poured themselves cups of coffee. There was plenty of tension in the air, and it had nothing to do with basic housekeeping. Some people made a point of sitting near the first group, like lurkers trying to get a seat near the popular kids in the school cafeteria. Others made a point of sitting far away. Everyone noticed me. Some smiled politely and others just ignored me altogether. That was until one of the men up front turned, looked over his shoulder and called across the room. "You're Sunni Taylor, aren't you? Prudence said she'd be sending her best reporter. Glad you're here," he said and turned toward the front.

My gaze crashed right into Tracy's glower. She tugged at

her coat again. It was tight, and it might have been inching up due to the rigidity in her shoulders. The empty seat next to me was suddenly taken.

"I decided this might be too interesting to miss," Lana muttered as she leaned her head closer to mine. She looked back at the coffee cart, then spun around and rested back. "As usual, terrible snack display. One of the reasons I don't bother to show up to these meetings."

I chuckled. "So, it's all about the snacks." I thought about it. "Actually, yeah, I can see that. When Prudence forgets to bring donuts or pastries to a Monday morning meeting, it feels like a gut punch, like she doesn't like us or want us to be happy. I guess they're not wasting dues on treats, eh?"

"I think the snacks come right out of Ralph's kitchen cupboard," Lana said.

"Ralph?" I asked. "Is he the slightly hunched man with the wire-framed glasses?"

"Yep, he's the secretary." As she said it, a tall, nice-looking man with splashes of gray in otherwise dark hair strolled in. He was buttoning his suitcoat as he walked through the room, and he caught everyone's attention.

"And that is Peter Zander," Lana whispered. "He's the president. He's a real estate broker."

"Yep, I've seen his face on billboards. 'We've got your housing needs covered from A to Zander,'" I recited.

"That's him. He rarely shows to these meetings. It's usually just Tracy and her little pet puppy dog, Ralph. She orders him around. All but tells him to *sit* and *stay*."

Ralph took a few minutes to fiddle with the projector while Tracy thumbed through a notebook. The society president,

Mr. Zander, sat at the table and instantly pulled out his phone. He was busy sending texts while Ralph got the projector running. Zander had nothing to say to Tracy and vice versa, and they sat at opposite ends of the table. It was Zander who finally called the meeting to order.

The last meeting's minutes were projected onto the screen.

"See how high-tech this operation is? I think they got that projector and screen from the school district warehouse where they keep out-of-date equipment," Lana quipped. "They could email those minutes. Not that any of us would open the emails."

Ralph scurried around to the table, sat down with a plunk and opened up his own notebook. He lifted a pen ready to record meeting notes. It reminded me that I should do the same.

"Let's hear the minutes from the last meeting," Zander said in a commanding voice. He looked even more impressive in person than on the billboards, and it was more than obvious that he had little or no interest in the meeting because after he asked for the minutes to be read, he pulled out his phone and busied himself with another text.

I leaned closer to Lana. "How did he become president?"

"No one else wanted the position. You get a nice plaque to hang on the wall of your office. Not sure if there are any other benefits."

"Don't bother, Ralph. We can read the minutes right there," a man in the original group said as he stood up and pointed at the screen.

Zander finally paused his personal phone chats to address the man. "Nathan, we need to follow protocol."

"No, we're here for one thing and one thing only, and with all due respect, Zander, you're never at these meetings, and far as we can tell you have no hand in this society except to be able to tell your clients that you're president of the Small Business Society."

Zander sat forward. "Now listen here, Nate—"

The rest of the original group stood up to support Nathan. Zander sat back. "What is this about?" he asked. He was suddenly meeker than seconds before.

"We're paying dues, hefty dues at that. Those are supposed to be collected and held in an account so that when one of us needs it, we have financial support through a difficult time." Nathan turned to the couple next to him. "Rick and Hannah, here, have fallen on hard times. They sell lawnmowers and garden supplies. When the city council passed the ordinance that gas-powered lawnmowers were going to be phased out and eventually banned, they were stuck with a lot of stock no one wanted. In addition, they needed funds to buy new electric-powered machines. When they asked for assistance from the society, they were turned down."

Zander looked down the table at Tracy. She'd been pretending to take her own notes—at least that was the impression I got. "Tracy, what is going on with their claim?" Zander was one of *those* leaders, the kind who paid no attention at all to his position and then stepped in occasionally to pretend he had an interest.

Tracy made a show of putting down her pen. She steepled her fingers together in front of her. "There was no medical or catastrophic emergency, so the funds were denied."

Loud protests erupted. One of the men stood and waved

his fist. "We need to know where our dues are going. Back when Leonard Forbes was in charge, we got a copy of the monthly budget so we knew exactly where the money was going. Ms. Goodwyn hasn't been providing us with anything. It's all secretive." He pointed his thumb to the back of the room. "There used to be pastries and donuts and coffees from the local coffee shop. Now we get the leftovers from Ralph's cookie jar."

"Told you," Lana mumbled.

A woman stood up. "For all we know Tracy could be spending the money on her expensive shoes. What'd those pumpkin orange ones cost ya, eh?"

Tracy's face was getting red, and she began to fidget with her notebook. Her gaze flashed my direction more than once. She figured this whole humiliating scene was going to be broadcast in the local paper, but I wasn't *that* kind of journalist. I'd never write a story until I knew all the facts. The question was—would Tracy be willing to share those facts?

Zander thumped the table with his fist to get everyone's attention. "Please sit down so we can solve this issue." The crowd reluctantly sat. Zander looked down the table at his treasurer. "Ms. Goodwyn, what is a reasonable amount of time needed for you to pull together a full budget breakdown for the last, let's say, three months?"

Tracy looked nearly nauseous. "Uh, it'll take me at least a week."

The protests started up again, but Zander kept control. "Every member needs a copy of the budget in their inboxes by one week from today. And since things are too tense today to hold a proper meeting, we'll adjourn and come together again in a week. By then, we'll have the budget in hand, and we can discuss it like proper business people."

People reluctantly stood up. Tracy got up quickly and hurried out of the room.

Lana looked over at me. "Did you get enough for a story?"

I looked down at my mostly empty notepad. "A headline maybe. A story, no. At least, not yet."

CHAPTER 10

The long day and brisk evening air had left me with a craving for cinnamon apple tea. Jackson brought home dinner from our favorite burger joint, and like a kid waiting to go outside and play, he vacuumed down his food and hurried out to see his horse. The dogs followed closely at his heels.

Edward hung back with me while I put the kettle on for tea. I glanced his direction. He was near the hearth looking pensive and a little sad.

"Uh-oh, Edward Beckett has something on his mind," I said.

"Nothing, really."

"That face doesn't say *nothing*. What's wrong? I'm planning to go outside with my tea. Care to join me? I think Jackson is going to give Cash some turnout time in the pasture before it's too dark."

"No, that's all right. You take your tea outside. I'll stay here."

The kettle whistled and I poured water into the cup. "You sound like you're feeling sorry for yourself." It was probably not the best comment given his mood.

"What could I possibly feel sorry about?" he asked with that dry tone that assured me more was coming. "I lost my life so early, I never saw my thirtieth birthday, and all because I was so befuddled from losing Kat that I lost my head and started down a path that led me to the aforementioned early death. Then, I find that I'm stuck here in this house for eternity where moments of joy are so few and far between that I don't even recognize those moments when they arrive."

I picked up my cup and walked closer to him. His emotions could push his image in either direction—wobbly and faded or clear and sharp as high-definition television. Tonight, it was so clear, I was sure if I reached out, I'd touch something solid.

"Edward, I didn't realize you were so miserable here…with me. I thought we had, you know, something that admittedly was complex but that came with its own moments of joy." I realized that his words had hurt me but then it was easy to see his point of view. Even the lovely cup of tea I was holding was a small joy that he'd never experience again.

"Of course, you do make my existence tolerable," he said.

"Tolerable," I repeated. "I'm not going to walk out of here starry-eyed from that compliment, but thank you. What's really got you in such a bad mood? Is it Cash?"

The clear image faded and disappeared completely. It was

very annoying that he could just vanish when he didn't like the discussion.

"Fine. Then brood on your own, but I'm going to go outside and watch the horse." I stopped at the back door and looked outside. Jackson was leading Cash around the yard. It seemed he was giving him a narrated tour. "You've got to see this, Edward. Jackson is leading the horse around the yard, pointing out different things, complete with descriptions." There was no response. I suspected that giving him time was the only thing that would lift him out of his dark mood. I reached for the door, and an idea popped into my head. I put down my tea and pushed out the door.

I hurried out to Jackson. He'd paused near the back of the house to let Cash graze on some grass that hadn't yet been ravaged by the cold night temperatures, so it was still green. Jackson looked up. He was wearing the smile that had been plastered on his face since Cash was unloaded from the trailer.

"Thought I'd let him see the whole yard," he explained.

"Yes, I noticed." I reached him. "Jax, I was wondering—would it be weird if we let Edward have a chance to sit on the horse."

Jackson's face snapped my direction. "Seriously?"

"Yeah. He's in there with that pouty face and those occasional melancholy sighs. Obviously, he wouldn't really be sitting on Cash's back but—"

"It might feel like it to him, like in a virtual reality game," Jackson finished.

"Exactly."

Jackson glanced toward the back stoop. "I can walk Cash over to the stoop. Go see if he wants to climb on."

I raced back to the house, excited that I'd come up with a brilliant plan. Now, would Edward consider it equally brilliant?

I burst into the house. "Edward! Edward?" He really was brooding. "Come outside. Jackson is going to walk Cash closer to the house, so you can climb on his back." Again, no response until "that's absurd" came from somewhere in the room.

"Is it? Because I think it could be awesome." I waited and listened in the empty room. No sign of Edward. "Fine, I thought it might bring you one of those easy-to-miss moments of joy, but I guess it was a silly idea." I stepped outside.

Jackson and Cash were standing near the back stoop. Jackson looked up expectantly. I shook my head.

"It's absurd, but I'm sure you won't stop bothering me about it, so I'll give it a try." Edward was standing next to me.

"You're right. Pesky old me will not let it drop until you sit yourself on that fine steed." Before I could finish, Edward had disappeared and reappeared on the horse's back.

Jackson and I stayed quiet. Edward was deep in his thoughts. He got that way whenever his past came back to him. He sat up straight and made such a fine figure it was hard to know who looked better on the horse—Edward or Jackson.

"His withers are very even, and his neck is strong and sturdy from up here," Edward finally said. He sat there for a long time. Jackson winked at me over Cash's back. For a few, nice moments Edward Beckett was alive again, sitting in his favorite place—on the back of a horse.

CHAPTER 11

*J*ackson hated having to work on Sunday, especially knowing that he wouldn't be spending the day with his horse, but several of the other detectives were out sick and he needed to cover for them.

I sat at the table with a plate of scrambled eggs and my mostly blank notebook. I'd let Prudence know that the Small Business Society budget issues would be delayed until next week. Tracy Goodwyn looked almost sick with the notion that she had to pull together the budget data by next week. It was her job as treasurer and shouldn't have been such a burden, but something told me there was far more to the story. At least, as a journalist covering it, I hoped that was the case. In the meantime, I had a few other stories on my computer that would work for this week's column. That meant I was free for the day.

Edward's mood had improved immensely after his moments on the horse. This morning he'd gone out to the back stoop with the dogs. Cash was in the barn, but Edward seemed to be reliving the moment as he stood and stared out at the landscape.

I stepped out onto the stoop. Redford and Newman were busy sniffing all the new horsey smells in the yard. "It's a shame Brady has to work today." Edward was one of the few people who called Jackson by his proper name. It always made me smile because it reminded me they were related. Sometimes, like right now, with the slightly misty sunshine highlighting Edward's handsome profile, I could see a family resemblance. Their genes had gone through many generations and many grafted branches on the family tree, but the two men had more in common than they realized. Like their love of horses.

"You enjoyed yourself last night," I said.

His broad, transparent shoulders vibrated with a shrug. "It was fine."

I laughed. "Fine? I was sure we'd be sitting out here until midnight. But I'm glad you're feeling better," I added quickly. My phone rang. I pulled it out of my pocket. "Oh, it's Emily."

"The less annoying sibling," Edward muttered.

"Hey, Emi, what's up?"

"Two things," Emily said. "One, and the best one at that, Nick brought home the mini donkeys last night. Arlo and Angel are here and waiting for a snuggle from their Auntie Sunni."

"Ahh! I can't wait to come snuggle them."

Edward glanced my direction, rolled his eyes and then disappeared.

"That brings me to the second thing. I need some help delivering pies to the Griswold mill. If you're not too busy—"

"Say no more. I'm on my way with snuggles packed and ready to be delivered." To say I was excited was an understatement. A friend of Nick's had to sell his farm to move to New York and take care of his aging parents. He had to find homes for his animals, and he'd promised his two miniature donkeys, Arlo and Angel, to Nick and Emily. Nick had been busily fixing a nice stall for the two donkeys, and it seemed the big day had arrived. I pulled on a sweatshirt and boots, the pair I'd bought for barn chores and for visiting Emily's farm. I was starting to feel like a real country girl.

"She's pulled on her boots," Edward drawled as I searched for my keys.

"The donkeys have arrived at Emily's farm, and I plan to instantly become their favorite aunt."

He appeared near the corner of the kitchen counter and pointed out my keys. "In my day, a donkey was only good for making a terrible racket, kicking unsuspecting people and carrying goods to market."

"And now they are bred for snuggling, which is something I'm very good at." I snatched up the keys. "Be back later." It was a short enough walk, but I was so excited I drove to Emily's.

The cold morning mist was starting to thin out, but the brilliant landscape colors had been muted by the gray moisture. With any luck, it would burn off by noon. Nick was stepping out of the chicken yard. He'd just fed them, so the birds didn't look up or do their usual clucking dance as I walked up.

"Where are they?" I asked.

Nick laughed. My sister's husband was the whole package: handsome, thoughtful, charming and always in a pleasant mood. My little sister deserved nothing less. "They're in their stall. I want to give them a day or two to get used to their new surroundings before I turn them out." Emily and Nick's Belgian mare, Butterscotch, was out in the pasture nibbling what was left of the summer grass. The two goats, Tinkerbell and Cuddlebug, were standing nearby, playfully headbutting each other.

"I think Butterscotch will be happy to have companions that aren't goats. Not that she minds Tinkerbell and Cuddlebug, but goats aren't the same as donkeys." Nick led the way to the barn.

Emily stepped out the back door. "Oh, I see how it is. Donkeys before sisters. I'm going to start boxing up the pies. Don't be too long. I don't want to be late delivering them."

I waved. "Just a few snuggles, I promise."

Nick and I reached the stall and standing inside were two of the most adorable little sweeties on the planet. "That's Arlo with the chocolate and white splotches, and Angel is the dun. They're both three years old." He opened the stall door.

I expected the two donkeys to move to the back of the stall. Instead, they trotted forward to greet me. I stroked their coats. "Their coats are so lush and thick, like a soft carpet." It didn't take long for them to realize I was a new friend. They let me snuggle and hug them. "I may have to get a pair for the farm," I said.

"How is Cash?" Nick asked.

"Jackson is over the moon. Cash is a great horse. Settled right in."

Emily joined us in the barn. She handed me a few treats to feed the donkeys. They ate them with enthusiasm. "There, my goal to be favorite aunt has been achieved." As much as I hated to leave the donkeys, I knew Emily was anxious to deliver her pies.

I held up my hands. "Guess I should wash up before I handle baked goods." We walked back to the house. The smell of cinnamon and buttery crust wafted around the kitchen. There was a massive pile of apple peels sitting on a tray ready to be tossed onto the compost heap; otherwise, aside from the heady aroma, it was impossible to tell that Emily had just baked two dozen pies.

I washed my hands. "Did you ever talk to Annie?" I asked.

"I finally got ahold of her. I wanted to make sure she was all right with me helping out. Of course, I plan to give the money to Annie." Emily handed me a dry towel.

"That's what I figured. How did she take the news?"

"She wasn't too pleased but then she told me she wanted nothing to do with the Griswolds, so I could bake the pies and we'd still be friends. Although there was a definite chill in her tone."

"That'll melt when you give her the money," I said. Emily didn't take well to people being angry with her. And it was nearly impossible to stay mad at my younger sister. She was just too likable.

A few minutes later we were in the truck and the boxed pies were sitting in the bed waiting for their trip to the mill. "It's a little ironic," I said as Emily started the truck. "We're bringing apples to a cider mill."

"Well, Amanda did provide me with the apples. They

weren't great apples. Some were so mealy I couldn't use them for the pies."

"Ah yes, then maybe Shawn Griswold had good reason to fire his produce man. I saw the two of them arguing outside the mill. Shawn told the guy with the Jonah's Produce hat that he was going to find a new produce man."

"Jonah's produce can be questionable. I think he buys bulk, and occasionally, his fruits and veggies are past their prime." The truck rolled down the gravel drive. "I'll be glad to be done with this chore. And I won't be doing it again. If Amanda wants pies baked, she's going to need to find a new baker."

CHAPTER 12

I hadn't said a word, but it was obvious Emily was feeling the same way as me. Something didn't seem right at the Griswold place. Firstly, it was eerily quiet. Aside from a few pigeons strolling through the yard searching for crumbs left behind by yesterday's visitors, the whole place was quiet. There was no sign of Shawn or Amanda.

"Kind of weird, right?" Emily asked.

"Yes, unless they both overslept. This place will be flooded with visitors in two hours. It seems like they should be hustling and bustling to get things ready. I don't see Tucker's truck either, but then maybe his shift doesn't start until later."

Emily drove the truck closer to the house. "I guess we can knock on the kitchen door before we pull all these boxes out of the truck."

We walked up to the kitchen door. It was quiet inside. Emily knocked twice, but there was no answer. "Very weird. I thought she'd be up early making those donuts. Maybe she gave up on that idea." She pulled out her phone and called Amanda. Emily shook her head. "Voicemail only. Hey, Amanda, I'm at the kitchen door with the pies." She hung up and looked around. "Maybe they're in the mill?"

"Just in case—" I reached for the doorknob. It turned.

Emily bit her lip, and her cute blonde brows bunched. "Feels like trespassing."

"Nonsense. We're delivering her pies, and she's not answering." I opened the door. The smell of cinnamon wafted toward us. I stepped inside the service porch. There were shelves filled with pantry items and beneath the shelves was a bench. Under the bench were pairs of shoes and work boots. I knocked on the doorway. "Hello? Amanda, it's Sunni and Emily. We have your two dozen pies." I caught a glimpse of something on the floor. It was a silver mixing bowl turned on its side. Cinnamon sugar was piled next to the bowl. It had spilled all over the floor. My instincts assured me something terrible had happened. I turned to Emily who had stayed tucked behind me, not out of fear but because she was still hesitant about entering a house uninvited.

"Emi, let me go into the kitchen alone." There was no way to make that statement sound less ominous.

Emily touched my arm lightly. "Do you think something's happened to the Griswolds?"

I nodded. "I'll take a look. Stay right here." I stepped around the corner wall and got a full view of the kitchen. Amanda Griswold was in a heap on the floor. She was wearing a pink checked apron and holding a rolling pin in her limp, white hand. Blood was pooled beneath her head. It didn't take long to find the source of the blood—a bullet hole near her temple. I'd seen enough dead bodies—unfortunately—to know that I was looking at a dead woman. I walked lightly through the kitchen, making sure to avoid the spilled cinnamon sugar. There was a footprint in the sugar. I crouched down next to Amanda and lightly pinched her wrist between my fingers and thumb. I didn't feel a pulse but then I was no medic. I pulled out my phone and dialed emergency services as I walked back toward Emily. I took a quick photo of the footprint before leaving the kitchen.

Emily's face was pale, and she was still biting her lip. She winced when she saw my expression. "Is she—"

I nodded. "Someone shot Amanda Griswold." As I said it, a jolt of fear and adrenaline shot through me. "Shawn."

Emily grabbed my hand. "Did he kill his wife? And if so—where is he?" her voice cracked. I put my arm protectively around her shoulders and led her quickly out of the house. I scanned the yard for any sign of Shawn. If he'd been inside the house, then he'd been as quiet as a mouse. It was even quieter out in the yard. That was when I noticed that the door to the mill was slightly ajar.

I hurried Emily to her truck. "Get inside, lock the door and be prepared for a fast getaway."

Emily climbed inside. She grabbed my hand. "You get in, too," she pleaded.

"I've already called for an ambulance and let them know a woman has been shot. I'm sure Jackson will be here soon. I'll text him to make sure. In the meantime, I'm just going to check out the mill."

"But what if Shawn is hiding out there with a gun?"

"My intuition tells me that's not the case," I assured her.

And it was true. Something told me the morning horror show wasn't over yet. "Remember, lock the door, and if you see me running toward the truck, get ready to go."

"Sunni, I'm scared."

I leaned into the truck and hugged her. "It'll be fine. I'll be right back."

I kept my eyes peeled for any movement. The banners and fall decorations shimmied in the slight breeze floating through the yard. I reached the mill door. It was a heavy wooden door complete with a big iron latch. This morning, the latch and the door hung open.

"Mr. Griswold?" I called inside. The smell coming out of the mill was sweet with a touch of fermentation. It was dark inside, and the gray mist outside didn't help. I turned on my phone flashlight. I startled when it vibrated in my hand. I glanced at the text from Jackson.

"What's going on?" he asked.

"The cider mill. Please hurry." That last part would alarm him, but I really needed him here. "Mr. Griswold?" I asked cautiously as I stepped farther into the mill. A massive pile of pomace, the pulp left behind after the apples had gone through the press, was heaped at the far end of the mill. Shawn Griswold was lying face down in the apple debris.

I aimed my somewhat pathetic light beam around the whole interior. The modern equipment had a few lights blinking, but it wasn't running. I walked to the ancient stone mill and shined my light into the corner behind it. I didn't want to be surprised by a killer lurking in the dark recesses of the mill. It seemed that other than the dead man in the pomace pile, the mill was empty.

I made my way around the historic presses and some crates of apples to the pomace. Blood had spilled into the pile of pulp. Shawn Griswold had suffered the same fate as his wife— a gunshot to the head.

"Sunni?" Emily's shaky voice echoed through the building.

I hurried toward her. "Emi, I told you to stay in the car."

"I was worried about you. Did you find him? Did you find Shawn Griswold?"

"I did. He's dead, too."

Emily's hand flew to her chest. "A double murder?"

"I'm afraid so."

She shook her head. "Who would do such a thing?" Her blue eyes held a good dose of fear. "And what if they're still here?" This time her hand flew to her mouth. "Do you think it was Raine's boyfriend, Tucker?"

"Way too early to make any guesses. From what I witnessed yesterday, during my short time at the mill, Shawn Griswold was not too well-liked and with good reason. He was a disagreeable person."

"But why kill Amanda, too?" Emily said. "She was a little vapid and selfish, but she was likable enough." Emily's eyes rounded. "Do you think Annie could have done this? When I talked to her, she had nothing but bad things to say about the Griswolds, especially Shawn."

Sirens cracked the misty air with their high-pitched squeals.

"Thank goodness the officials are on their way," Emily said. "Is there a chance that either of them is still alive?"

"I'm not a doctor, but I'd say no chance at all. They were

both shot in the head." That comment made the color drain from Emily's face.

I took hold of her arm and led her outside for some fresh air. The red lights were visible now. The mill was on a quiet road where their neighbors were few and far between. It was the perfect remote location for a double homicide. And in our short time in the mill, Emily, someone who'd never dabbled in a murder investigation, had already offered up two possible suspects. Both notions seemed farfetched, but one never knew what was bubbling and brewing behind someone's anger. The Griswolds had treated their employees and even their produce man badly. Was it one of them or someone else who might have had a grudge? Something told me the list of characters would be long on this one.

CHAPTER 13

I readily sent my very shaken sister home…with her pies. She had no idea what to do with two dozen pies, but it seemed the cider mill's season opener had ended in catastrophe. There would be no cider sipping, no apple pies and no mill demonstrations today. The ambulance had arrived first, and the medics confirmed what I already knew—Shawn and Amanda Griswold were dead. Jackson had been in Birch Highlands handling a domestic dispute, so it took him longer than expected to arrive. Once he pulled up, my whole body relaxed in relief. It wasn't my first murder scene, but a double murder was especially horrific. The pair were not all that likable, but they didn't deserve this.

Jackson got out of the car, and his broad shoulders softened when he saw me. The first thing he did was pull me into his strong arms for a hug, and I wasn't about to complain. In fact, his embrace was just what I needed for fortification after the terrible morning.

"Dispatch said a man and woman are dead," he said as we walked toward the mill. The paramedics were stepping out the heavy door with their equipment and gurney. They were no longer needed at the scene. The coroner would need to take over from here.

"Two confirmed deaths," one of the medics said as we reached them.

"Thanks. I'll call the coroner," Jackson told them. I followed him inside the mill.

"Emily and I drove out here to deliver the apple pies Emi baked for today's event. We knew almost immediately that something was wrong. There was no answer at the kitchen door, and Amanda wasn't answering her phone. The kitchen door was unlocked." I paused and looked at him wide-eyed. "I touched the door handle. I'm sorry. I didn't realize there'd been a murder."

Jackson shook his head. "Don't worry. Like you said, you had no idea what was waiting for you inside. If this was a planned murder, which I suspect was the case, then the killer probably came prepared with gloves." Jackson walked over to the pile of apple pulp and stared down at Shawn Griswold. "Looks like we've got a mess to deal with." He pulled out his phone to call the coroner.

"I'm going to head into the house and look around." I held out my palm. He knew what I wanted without asking. He rolled his eyes, but in a humorous way, before placing two latex gloves in my hand.

"Thank you, Detective Jackson, and I will use my utmost discretion as I browse through the house." I didn't look forward to spending time in the kitchen with a dead body but such was the life of an investigator. Before I stepped inside, I called to check on Emily. She answered in one ring.

"Sunni, did Jax arrive? I don't think you should stay there alone. What if the killer is still on the property?"

"Jax is here, so all is well. I was just calling to check on my little sister."

"Oh, well, I'm knee-deep in apple pies now, and I won't be paid for my labor." She gasped. "Gosh, what a terrible thing to say. The poor woman is dead, and I'm worried about the money."

"It's not terrible. You worked hard on those pies when I'm sure you had plenty of other things to do."

"Still, I'm only stuck with a bunch of pies. At least I'm not—well—you know. Does Jackson have any ideas about the case yet?"

"Too early. He'll wait for the coroner team and then evidence will be collected. I'm just heading back into the house to look around."

"In the house with the dead body?" Emily asked.

"Unless Amanda got up and walked out, yes, in the house with the body."

"I always forget that, for you, seeing a dead body is like seeing a sparrow land on a tree. I didn't actually see either Griswold, but I don't ever want to be that close to a dead body again."

"I will try and make sure it never happens. I'm heading inside now, so I'm going to hang up."

Emily chuckled lightly. I was glad to hear her getting back to her old self. "Are you worried Amanda will overhear our conversation?" She gasped again. "My gosh, I'm a ghoul. I need to take a nap. I was up too late baking pies. I think I'll drive them over to the soup kitchen in Smithville. I'm sure they can use some apple pies."

"I'm sure their patrons will appreciate them. Talk to you later, Emi." I hung up the phone and pulled on the gloves before I touched the doorknob. Not that it mattered now since my prints were clearly wrapped around it already, but there was no need to make it worse.

The cinnamon aroma had faded some, and it was now mixed with the unpleasant smell of blood. As I walked through the service porch area something ground under my shoes, something that felt like sand. I moved my feet and stooped down. I pressed my latex-covered finger against the grit and brought it to my nose to smell. It was cinnamon sugar. I'd made a point of avoiding the spilled mess on the floor, so it wasn't from *my* shoe.

I walked into the kitchen and crouched down closer to the pile of spilled cinnamon sugar. The large impression in the middle of it hadn't been disturbed, but it wasn't a clear print. Cinnamon sugar, like fine sand, was not good at holding the shape of a print. Still, I'd bet a big sum of money that the imprint in the middle of the spilled sugar was a footprint.

It occurred to me that Amanda herself might have made the print in the sugar, so I walked over and crouched down next to her feet. She was wearing rubber-soled work shoes, the kind with a thick tread that kept you from slipping on a wet kitchen spill. I couldn't find one speck of sugar on her shoes.

I stood up in the place where her feet must have been before she died. According to my calculations, she was standing at her worktable. A lump of yeasty-smelling donut dough was still sitting in the middle of a floured section of the table. The dough had spread and grown more bubbly and far less structured in the last hour as the yeast was doing its thing. It was at a stage that Emily would refer to as over-proofed. According to my expert sister, if you let a yeast dough rise too long, the resulting baked good would be flat and hard. A long, flour-dusted rolling pin was still resting in Amanda's hand. The bowl of cinnamon sugar must have fallen off the same worktable, and it was at a rolling pin's distance from Amanda's feet. I did a quick reenactment. I pretended to hold a rolling pin and faced the table. Amanda probably heard the back door open. She turned and the pin would've turned with her. It knocked the cinnamon sugar off the counter, and before she could fight her attacker off or drop the pin, she was shot in the head. She dropped to the floor where she stood. That made sense with a gunshot to the head. Death would likely be quick, instant, in fact.

The unlocked back door and the cinnamon sugar in the service porch all but confirmed my theory. The killer stepped in the mess and then tracked some of it on their way back to the door. If Shawn had been in the mill with its thick walls and noisy machinery, then it was likely he never heard the shot, assuming Amanda was the first victim.

I continued around the worktable to the rest of the kitchen. It seemed the Griswolds had taken down a few walls to make a vast kitchen. The area where Amanda was killed was set up commercially with stainless steel worktables, large sinks and multiple ovens. The other side of the kitchen was far homier, with checkered tile, an antique stove complete with enameled teapot, a small, scarred pine table and the obligatory rooster clock. There was even a rooster-shaped cookie jar on the counter near the stove.

The killer finished his deadly deed quickly, at least according to my theory, so it was hard to reason why he'd have gone any farther into the kitchen, but I took a quick tour around to make sure I didn't miss anything. The only thing that seemed out of place in the kitchen was a piece of paper jammed under the cookie jar. It seemed like an odd place to leave a grocery list, unless, of course, you needed reminding to buy cookies at the store. (I doubted many people needed *that* reminder.)

I pulled the paper out and unfolded it. There were two identical columns of numbers, but the totals at the bottom were quite different, by thousands. The lower total was circled in red, and by doing some quick math in my head, I determined it was the wrong total. There were no other marks on the paper. I took a photo of it and stuck it back under the cookie jar.

I heard car tires on gravel and glanced out the kitchen window. The coroner had arrived. It was time to leave the crime scene to the experts. I smiled to myself. I wasn't an expert, but I'd discovered the victims, and I had a short history here at the cider mill. I intended on solving this murder with or without the officials. It'd make for a great story.

CHAPTER 14

I waited around to hear what the coroner had to say. Jackson emerged from the kitchen where the team was finishing up. "Well, no surprise here," Jackson said. "They died between the hours of five and eight and in very close succession, though it's hard to tell who died first. We considered the possibility that Shawn killed his wife and then walked out to his mill to commit suicide, but he'd washed crates of apples and readied his equipment as if he planned to get to work. Seems like a strange thing to do if you're planning to go out in a murder-suicide. Plus, his wound didn't appear to be self-inflicted. However, since the gun was stuffed into the apple pulp—"

I stood up straighter. "You found the murder weapon?"

"Oh, didn't I say? Yes, it was shoved into the apple pulp next to Shawn Griswold."

"It's called pomace—the pulp, that is. Learned that yesterday in Tucker's demonstration." Saying his name reminded me that he hadn't shown up yet. Word wasn't out yet, but Jackson had called in several patrol cars to block off the road and turn back people planning to attend the event. There would be no festivities today, that was for darn sure. "So, where is the weapon?"

"On its way to forensics. Hopefully, we can trace it to the owner. It might even belong to Griswold. From what I can tell, the man was caught by surprise, took a bullet to the head and fell where he stood. It just happened to be next to the pile of apple—of pomace," he corrected.

"I theorized the same thing with Amanda, only she fell on her kitchen floor and managed to push a bowl of cinnamon sugar off the counter with the rolling pin she was holding. Did the team notice the impression in the middle of the spilled sugar?"

"We spotted that and some of the sugar was tracked to the back door."

I deflated some. "Poo, it seems like you guys were on top of it all today."

Jackson smiled. "Well, we are the people who get paid for it. Did you notice anything else in the house?"

"I never went past the kitchen. There was a piece of paper under the cookie jar with some numbers on it, but I'm not sure it's connected."

Jackson nodded. "Yeah, we picked that up too."

"Of course you did," I said, disappointedly.

The sound of a loud motor pulled Jackson's attention toward the parking area. "Who's that?"

I turned that way. "That's Tucker Carmichael, Raine's boyfriend. He's the handyman here at the mill. I was wondering if he was going to show up soon. The Griswolds treated him poorly," I managed to mutter before Tucker reached us.

Tucker looked more than bewildered about all the official-looking vehicles. It took him a second to recognize me. "Sunni, what's going on? There were police at the end of the road. I had to let them know that I worked here at the cider mill, and still, they were reluctant to let me cross their barricade."

"Tucker, this is Detective Jackson."

Tucker smiled. "Right, Raine has spoken about you. Nice to meet you." He glanced around at the cars. "Has something happened?"

Jackson nodded. "I need to speak with you, Mr. Carmichael. Amanda and Shawn Griswold are dead."

Tucker's face blanched. I offered him an arm, and he grabbed it to steady himself. It seemed like a genuinely shocked reaction to the terrible news. Jackson gave me the look that told me he'd be talking to Tucker alone. I'd seen a few neighbors gathering out on the road and decided to stroll down and talk to them. I usually found out more from nosy neighbors than from anyone else.

"I'll let you two talk," I said and took off toward the road.

The uniformed officers had been doing a great job keeping cars and spectators off the road, but there wasn't much they could do about the people who already lived near the mill. There were only a few farms on the section of road, so I was sure everyone knew each other, even if they weren't necessarily friends. Sometimes in a small community, it was better not to become close friends. That way awkwardness could be avoided if two neighbors suddenly had a disagreement.

APPLE CIDER ASSAULT

There were two women and a man standing straight down from the Griswold's home. The man was wearing a camouflage jacket and matching hat, and the two women wore coats and scarves.

The woman with black wavy hair and a plum-colored hat approached me first. "What's going on? I live in that yellow farmhouse at the end of the road. I've never seen so many official vehicles in one place. Sam, here, was telling us it must be something very grave."

Sam and the other woman reached us. He adjusted his cap. "Was I right? Did someone get killed? That mill equipment is dangerous," Sam continued as if he already knew the whole story. "I guess it wasn't Tucker who fell in. I just saw him pull up in his truck, and he looked more than a little confused by the scene."

"It's true there has been a death," I said.

The women gasped. "Shawn's dead?" the other woman asked. "I'm Megan, Sam's wife. We live on the first farm on the right. Are you with the police?" she asked.

"No, I was here to deliver some apple pies for today's festivities."

"Sam and I were hoping to drop by today for cider," Megan said. She clucked her tongue and shook her head. "Poor Amanda. She must be devastated."

I decided it wasn't my place to add to the bad news. They'd hear all the details soon enough.

Megan turned to the other woman. "Carol, you said you thought you heard a gunshot this morning."

This new revelation caused my ears to perk. "Is that right?"

"Yes, it was the strangest thing. I was brushing my teeth,

and I heard a bang. I told myself it was just Shawn doing target practice." Her brows jumped up. "Is that what happened? Was Shawn practicing with his gun? Did he accidentally shoot himself?"

"I'm sure the police will fill you in on the details. They'll want to talk to all of you since your farms are close by. Shawn owns a gun?" I asked to make certain.

"Sure does," Sam said and patted his camouflage jacket. "We occasionally went hunting together. He had a few pistols, too. He wasn't an avid collector or anything like that, but you can't be too careful out here. It's fairly remote."

"Yes, that makes sense." I spotted Jackson and Tucker heading toward the house, and my curiosity kicked into high gear. "It was nice meeting you all, and I'm sure the police will take statements soon." I hurried back toward the house and picked up my pace to catch the men.

Jackson heard me running up from behind.

I gave him my pleading smile, so he'd let me enter with them. "You'll want to talk to the neighbors. One of them heard a shot this morning," I said as I followed them inside. "Also, Shawn does have guns."

"Yes, that's what Tucker confirmed. We're going in to check if his gun safe is open."

We walked through the house. The coroner's team was getting ready to move Amanda to the black body bag for transport to the morgue. "Are there next of kin to contact?" I asked. "The neighbors have already theorized that Shawn is dead. They don't know about Amanda, but I'm sure news will get out soon."

"That's always the case these days with social media. And bad news travels faster than the speed of light," Jackson said.

"I know Shawn has a twin brother and a cousin," I added.

"Already got that information," Jackson said with a wry smile.

"Of course, Detective Jackson, carry on then." I shot him a secretive wink. Tucker was quiet and seemed to be moving in a thick fog. This whole thing had really shocked him, and rightly so.

"The safe is in his office," Tucker said. He led us into a small, wood-paneled study. Two filing cabinets sat on either end of a large desk. In the corner was a tall metal safe with a digital lock. It was shut tight.

Tucker sighed. "Sorry, I don't have the combination. But I know he had two pistols and a hunting rifle because I've seen the safe open."

Jackson nodded. "Thanks, you've been a great help." We headed back out. "I'll call you if I have other questions," he said to Tucker.

"I can go home then?" Tucker asked.

"Yes."

Tucker walked back to his truck.

"What's next, Detective? I find myself entirely at leisure today."

"You mean other than discovering multiple bodies?" Jackson asked.

"Yes, other than that."

"Well, I've got to notify next of kin."

"Great, I'll go, too," I said enthusiastically. Before he could say no, I spoke up. "I know a few things that might give you a list of suspects."

"Why am I not surprised?"

"Yep, and I can tell you all about them on the way to Riley Griswold's house."

Jackson glanced at his notebook. "How did you—" He shook his head. "Never mind. Silly question."

CHAPTER 15

The morning mist had lifted, and even though it had been a dark, grim morning, as far as dead bodies were concerned, it was turning out to be a glorious autumn day. The maples along the road glittered gold in the sunshine as we drove to Birch Highlands, where Riley Griswold, the victim's twin brother lived.

"You mentioned some suspects." Jackson pulled my attention from the fabulous fall landscape.

"Yes, there were two incidents at the mill yesterday. I have no idea if either means anything. The first is the reason behind Emily's and my visit to the mill this morning. Yesterday, while we ate lunch, smoke started billowing out of the farmhouse kitchen. It turned out Annie Blair, the woman who baked the pies and donuts for the mill, had taken a quick break, and she managed to burn a half-dozen pies. It wasn't really her fault because she hadn't had a break all morning. Shawn was so angry he fired her on the spot. Annie told Emily they were terrible people to work for, and she was just as glad not to have anything to do with them anymore. Tucker also confirmed that they were not an easy pair to work for, especially Shawn."

Jackson nodded. "He mentioned that when we spoke."

I looked over at Jackson. "Raine really likes Tucker. You don't think he had anything to do with this, do you?"

"If so, he put on a convincing act about being shocked by the whole thing. It's too early to check off suspects, and Tucker had access to all the areas at the mill. He also had a motive if you can consider working for terrible people motive. It does happen. An employee gets pushed to the limit, and they decide to get revenge. So, Annie Blair, right? I'll put her on my list."

"And then there was the incident with Jonah, the produce man," I started.

The name caused Jackson's face to turn my direction. "Jonah Dowd?"

"Tall, thin man with a sort of permanent scowl?" I asked.

"That's him. I've had to deal with him before. He has a bad gambling addiction and constantly finds himself in trouble with some of the local bookies. What happened in the incident?"

I sat up straighter, thrilled to have something significant to add to the case. "I overheard Shawn arguing with someone while I was standing inside the mill listening to Tucker's demonstration. I stepped out to see what was happening. Shawn was telling Jonah that his apples were bad and mealy and that he was going to find another produce provider. Jonah was mad. He stormed off with his crates of apples, leaving Shawn short on inventory."

"Guess I'll start with Jonah after I talk to Shawn's brother."

"By the way, they're identical twins, but Tucker indicated that the two brothers are not terribly close. The mill was an inheritance, but Riley wanted nothing to do with it so Shawn bought him out. Riley is in the landscaping business."

Jackson chuckled. "It's amazing how much information you collect in a short trip to the mill."

"Reporter, remember?" I grinned at him.

Riley lived in a small brick house at the end of a tree-lined street. As expected, his house was beautifully landscaped with nicely sculpted shrubs and rose bushes. A birdbath sat under a sprawling buckeye and a few jays were taking sips of water. The house was slightly shabby, but the front yard belonged in a magazine.

Jackson and I reached the door and knocked. It took a minute or so for the door to open. It was a little off-putting to see a man who looked exactly like the man with his head in the pomace. I'd already noted before that Riley was less neatly groomed than his brother. Shawn seemed the type to be fastidious with his appearance. Riley was the opposite, especially this morning. He was wearing a faded green robe, open, over a t-shirt and running shorts. I assumed he'd just pulled them on to answer the door. Dark beard stubble covered his jaw, and his hair was in disarray from a long night of sleep. Aromatic steam curled up from the cup of coffee in his hand. He didn't look like someone who'd committed two murders this morning, but maybe the fresh-out-of-bed look was on purpose.

"Can I help you?" he asked.

Jackson flashed his badge, and it instantly took some of the color out of Riley's face. "Riley Griswold?" Jackson asked. Not that there was any doubt that the man in front of us was next of kin, but Jackson had to ask.

"Yes, that's right. What's this about?"

"I'm afraid I have some news. Can we talk inside?" Jackson asked.

Riley was reluctant at first, then he backed out of the way to let us in. "If this is about those work permits, they're all up-to-date now."

"This isn't about work permits," Jackson said grimly. We stepped into the front room, but Riley didn't offer us a seat. He set his coffee down on an end table, tightened the belt around his robe and looked at each of us with a serious brow.

"I'm sorry to have to tell you, Mr. Griswold, but your brother, Shawn, and his wife, Amanda, have been found dead."

Riley stared at Jackson for a second as he absorbed the news. "Why, that's impossible," he finally said with a dry, cracked tone. He smiled weakly. "I was just at the mill yesterday. I spoke to both of them. They were busy with the season opener."

"I'm afraid it's true. The coroner is transporting both of them to the morgue as we speak."

"The coroner? The morgue?" He reached blindly back for the arm of the couch and then managed to find his way to a cushion. He sat down with a plop. "How is this possible? What happened? Was it some sort of accident?" He rubbed his face. "How can it be? I just spoke to them."

"Can I get you something?" I asked. "A glass of water?"

"Uh, no, thank you. Please, explain what happened."

I was no expert, well, not in the official sense, but his reaction of shock and grief seemed genuine. Then again, he might have just spent the last few hours practicing this reaction. If he had killed his brother and sister-in-law, then he knew for certain that the police would show up at his door. Maybe the robe and coffee were all part of the act. It was, after all, almost noon. Most people had shed their robes and pajamas by this time.

"I can't go into details, but we're considering it a double homicide," Jackson said.

Riley sat back as if all the muscles had gone out of his body. "Murder? How can that be? I mean my brother was good at ruffling feathers, but murder—and Amanda as well. This can't be true."

"I'm afraid it is true. I can see that you're in shock, so I'll return at a later hour to ask you a few questions," Jackson said. "But one quick one before we leave—"

I really was getting good at this because I knew exactly what he was going to ask.

"Where were you between the hours of five and eight this morning?" Jackson asked Riley.

Riley's brows moved up and down in slight dismay. "Well, I think that should be obvious." He pointed out his robe. "I was sleeping. I had a few beers and watched television late last night. I'm usually up at the crack of dawn for work, so I allow myself a few hours of extra sleep on Sunday mornings."

He certainly had that explanation ready to go.

"And you live here alone?" Jackson asked.

"Yes." His expression turned grim. "I guess now I'm really alone. Shawn was my only sibling, and our parents died five years ago, just a few months apart."

"You have a cousin," I reminded him.

"Yes, several, but only Tracy is local. I'll have to call her. She'll be shocked."

"I'll talk to you later, and again, we're very sorry," Jackson said as we reached the front door.

We stepped out into the crisp air and headed to the car.

"Well, what did you think?" I asked.

"Hmm, well, his alibi seemed a little too detailed and rehearsed, and I'm not sure I'm buying the robe and coffee at noon thing. And while there was shock, there was little grief."

I smiled. "I'm getting pretty good at this because those were my thoughts exactly."

"Great, pretty soon I'll hand you the badge, and I'll stay home all day with my horse. And here I was hoping this would be a short workday."

CHAPTER 16

"I'm enjoying having a partner today," Jackson said. "And I'm also thinking about lunch."

"When aren't you thinking about lunch?" I reminded him.

"Good point. We can grab a bite to eat after we talk to Jonah." Jonah's produce stand was right off Butternut Crest. I recognized it as soon as we pulled onto the dirt lot. I was lucky enough to have an endless supply of fresh produce from Emily and Nick's vegetable patch, but the Busy Bee Produce Stand was a popular stop for locals and passing tourists.

"I've driven past this stand many times, but I'm spoiled with farm fresh produce every day of the year, so I've never pulled off to shop here." I zipped up my coat. The afternoon breeze had a glacial bite to it.

"This is probably the last few weeks of the stand being open," Jackson said. "Jonah's wife, Sue, usually shuts the whole operation down before the first snow."

A woman wearing a denim shirt and gray pants was piling a basket high with apples. Something told me they were the very same apples that Jonah had carried away from the mill. Shawn had been quite upset that Jonah had the nerve to cart away his apples after Shawn insulted them.

Sue had short red hair. A soft gray headband covered her ears and kept the hair off her face. She smiled tentatively when she saw Jackson. If he'd dealt with Jonah and his forays into the underground world of illegal gambling, then seeing the detective probably signaled that her husband was, once again, in trouble. This time he might be in much deeper trouble than placing an illegal bet.

Sue placed two more apples in the basket, wiped her brow with the back of her hand and then brushed her palms together. "What's he been up to now?" she asked.

"Nothing, but is he around?" Jackson asked.

"No, he's still out on deliveries." She squinted an eye at him. "Don't tell me you came out here just to say hello."

Jackson smiled. "Not exactly. I need to talk to him about Shawn and Amanda Griswold."

Sue rolled her eyes. She had sparkly blue ones to contrast with her red hair. "Those two. Jonah was really angry with them yesterday. I guess Shawn insulted the quality of our produce, and it was loud enough for a lot of our regular customers to hear. What have they done now? They already fired him. I'm not sure what else they could do."

It seemed Jackson was going to keep the big "ta-da" moment to himself. Sometimes he did that when he wanted to ask questions without people getting defensive.

"There's been some trouble at the mill." It was a gentle

way to put it. "Do you know where Jonah was this morning from five until eight?"

She shrugged. "This morning? He downed a plate of eggs, and I filled his thermos with coffee. He left the house just after six. Then, he went out to deliver produce. A lot of the local restaurants schedule their deliveries for Sunday morning before the places open for brunch."

"So, the last time you saw him was just after six?" Jackson asked. "Does he have anyone working with him on the truck?"

A dry laugh spurted from her mouth. "We barely make enough to keep ourselves housed and fed. We certainly can't afford an employee."

Something told me Jonah's gambling problem hadn't helped their financial situation. Losing a client like Shawn Griswold would probably take a toll as well.

A loud truck vibrated the cold air and caused the top of the produce stand to shake. "You can talk to him yourself," Sue said. "There he is."

Similar to Tucker's, Jonah's truck was also very loud. A few of the nearby birds took off from their perches. Jonah's long, lean form stretched up from the truck. He shut the door and looked perturbed about his visitors.

"Detective Jackson," he said coldly. "What's going on? Is this about the Griswolds?"

Sue looked in question at Jackson. "Did something happen to the Griswolds?"

Jonah looked to Jackson to answer the question. It was obvious he'd already heard the news.

"Shawn and Amanda Griswold were found dead this morning," Jackson said.

Sue gasped. "Dead? My lord, how awful. Jonah, did you know?" There was the slightest tremble in her tone as if she worried her husband had had some hand in it.

"I heard the news while I was out delivering." Jonah turned to Jackson. "It figures you'd come straight here looking for me. I might be a gambler, but I'm not a killer."

Jackson wasn't thwarted by his early defense. "Do you own a gun?"

Jonah's lips rolled in, and his nostrils flared. He took a deep breath. "Yes, I do. I carry cash because that's how some of my customers like to pay. So, I keep a loaded handgun under the driver's seat. I can show it to you. I didn't kill them."

"We can check for the gun in a second." It was obvious Jackson had dealt with Jonah more often than he cared to, and he wasn't bothering with any politeness or niceties. "Where were you between the hours of five and eight this morning?"

"Ate breakfast around six, then I left for my deliveries."

Jackson pulled out a notepad. "I need the names of the places you delivered, so I can verify your alibi."

Jonah huffed. "Fine." He looked flustered. "After I left the house this morning, I drove up to the mountains, to the East Fork trailhead. I sat in the truck and drank my coffee. I needed a little time to clear my head before I started my workday."

Jackson peered up at him with a touch of suspicion. "What time were you at the trailhead?"

"Got there about half past six and sat there for about forty-five minutes. I got to Bill's Diner about a quarter till eight. They were my first stop. And before you ask—no one saw me up at the trail unless you count the fox that ran past with the mouse in his snout."

"Let's check for that gun," Jackson said.

"Right." Jonah took heavy steps back to the truck. "You're wasting your time here. I didn't kill them." He ducked into his truck and emerged with a handgun. "You can take it if you like. You'll see it hasn't been fired since the last time I was at the shooting range."

"That won't be necessary," Jackson said. "Just need your list of customers this morning, and we'll be on our way."

Jonah pulled a list out from his truck, and Jackson wrote down a few names.

"I hear that Shawn fired you yesterday," Jackson said as he finished his notes. "I'm sure that made you mad."

"Of course it did, but I'm just as glad not to be working for them. Griswold was always complaining. Even if I went out of my way to get him his produce early, he never said thanks. There are probably a lot of people you could be talking to about his death, but I'm not one of them. As you know, I've had a few stints behind bars, and I don't ever plan to land there again. Especially not over a man like Griswold. Like I said—just as glad not to have to deal with him anymore."

"Right, well, I've got these names, and I'm sure they'll check out. Thanks for your time."

Jackson and I headed back to his car.

"Well?" I asked.

"Well, he almost had a solid alibi. Too bad he decided to take a detour to the mountains."

"But the gun was obviously not his," I said.

"Unless he owns more than one."

"Ahh, see that's why you get paid for this, and I'm just a cute sidekick."

Jackson laughed. "That you are. In fact, you might just be the cutest partner I've ever had."

I looked at him over the top of the car. "Might?"

"Okay, you're definitely in the top three. Now get in. I'm starved."

CHAPTER 17

Jackson and I bought sandwiches and took our lunch to the park. It was colder than I'd anticipated, but it was still a lovely afternoon. "Today already feels like it's been days long. This was supposed to be my day of rest."

Jackson had done his usual vacuum job on his sub sandwich, and he'd spent the rest of our lunch break scrolling through his phone. He didn't look up from the screen.

I wadded up the wrapper from my sandwich and then cleared my throat. "Hello, sixteen-year-old Brady Jackson. Earth to Jax."

Jackson put down the phone. "Sorry. I was looking for a better saddle pad. The one I'm using slips around too much."

"Well, I hate to take you out of the equine world, but where to next, partner?"

Jackson pulled out his notepad. "Bill's Diner and then over

to the Cluck and Coffee. Mostly we're going there to make sure Jonah is telling the truth about doing deliveries this morning. If those check out, we'll be able to end the verification there because the next stop was at nine o'clock at the Pancake House, and we know the victims were already long dead by then."

"I think it was barely eight when Emily and I reached the mill."

"That helps narrow down the window of time to between five and well before eight. You're certain you didn't see anyone driving down that road when the two of you reached the mill?"

I rubbed my temple to think back to this morning. I shook my head. "No, I don't remember seeing anyone on the road or leaving the mill. The killer was already gone by the time we pulled up to the house."

"Thank goodness," he muttered. "That shrinks the time frame even more. Unfortunately for Jonah, the hole in his alibi just happens to coincide with the time of the murders."

We got up from the park table, tossed our trash and headed back to the car. "When will you go back to talk to Riley? I'm still wondering if that fresh-out-of-bed look was staged. And like you said—there wasn't much grief. Not a tear, in fact. I know some men are reluctant to cry, but if your twin brother and his wife are murdered, you'd expect at least a sniffle."

"But what motive would Riley have to kill his own brother? If Shawn bought out Riley's share of the mill, then there was no inheritance feud."

"Maybe there's something else in their history," I

suggested. "Tucker told me the two brothers weren't close." We climbed in the car, and something else struck me. "Shawn's cousin, Tracy Goodwyn. I just remembered a third incident at the mill, only this one didn't include Shawn. It was with Amanda. Tracy was at the event—in her very impractical high heels—" I waved that detail off. "Not important. I couldn't make out what they were saying, but Tracy and Amanda had words, contentious words. I could tell by their postures and expressions. It just so happens I'm supposed to be covering a problem at the Small Business Society, some fuzzy budget numbers, and Tracy is the treasurer. I don't know how any of that could be connected to the murders, but I thought I should mention it."

Jackson took out his notebook and wrote down the name Tracy Goodwyn. He started the car. "Let's go to Bill's Diner and check Jonah's alibi. Then, I want to go back to the mill. The team couldn't find any cell phones. Neither victim was carrying one. There was so much activity with two murder scenes, they were probably just overlooked."

"Good plan, partner." I winked at him. "You know something? I think you're in my top three of cute partners, too."

Jackson laughed as he pulled the car onto the road. Bill's Diner was comprised of two old railroad cars connected together. The inside was cheery with black-and-white checkered flooring, peach-colored seating and white bell-shaped pendant lights hanging over each table. The sign out front boasted that they served breakfast all day, and today's special was cinnamon-apple pancakes. I'd had about enough apples for an entire season after this morning's crime scenes.

Bill had owned the diner for years and his partner, Tim,

helped him run the place. The Sunday brunch crowd had come and gone, and the two men were chatting as Bill filled ketchup bottles and Tim wiped down the tables. Tim saw us first. "Take any table you like, but I must warn you, we ran out of bacon."

Jackson had his badge ready. "Just here to ask a few questions."

Bill put down his big jug of ketchup, wiped his hands on his apron and circled around to the dining area to join us. "Detective Jackson, what's going on? Does this have anything to do with what happened at the mill? Tim and I know the Griswolds, but not well," he added apparently deciding to get that fact out there from the start.

"So, it's true, then," Tim said. "They were murdered."

Jackson didn't answer directly, but he didn't deny it either. He pulled out his notepad. "Just checking a few facts. Did you get a delivery from Jonah Dowd this morning?"

They both looked at each other with wide eyes. "Yes, Jonah delivered some apples and potatoes this morning," Bill confirmed.

"He was a little late," Tim added. "I was waiting in the back for his delivery. He usually arrives around a quarter past seven. I think he got here at half past seven."

"Well, I mean the time does vary." Bill added. He gave Tim a somewhat scolding look.

Tim smiled. "That's true. He's not always on time. We didn't hear the news about the Griswolds until later. Jonah mentioned that he and Shawn had parted ways and that he was no longer delivering apples to the mill."

"How did Jonah seem to feel about that?" I asked.

"He was upset about losing the revenue, but he was also relieved not to have to work with Shawn anymore," Bill said. "I've heard he can be difficult, but like I said, we didn't know the Griswolds well."

"Thanks for your help." Jackson put away his notepad. The two men watched us leave and then jumped right into conversation when we walked out.

"I think that quick visit just sparked a long strand of rumors. Jonah isn't going to be happy," I said.

"He'll be fine. He has a tough skin. I think we can skip the Cluck and Coffee. The time frame doesn't fit. We know he was at least telling the truth about his delivery schedule, but it still doesn't fill in that time gap when he was allegedly up at the trailhead."

We got in the car. The afternoon temperature had dropped enough that I was relieved to get inside the warm car. "If I didn't know any better, I'd think you were looking hard at Jonah as a suspect. Is that because he's already been in trouble with the law?"

"No, although that does sometimes play into it. It's just that—why go up to the mountains to clear his head? If I've got a truck filled with produce and my customers are waiting for their deliveries, then why take 'me time' in the middle of it all?"

"Maybe he was still dealing with the anger and disappointment of losing a customer? But I agree, Jonah doesn't seem like the stop-and-smell-the-roses type."

Jackson released a sigh. He'd been hoping for a short workday, and now, it seemed, it was going to be longer than ever. "Let's go back to the mill and find those phones. Maybe we'll get lucky and someone sent a threatening text before they showed up with a gun."

"That's looking on the bright side of things."

CHAPTER 18

My phone rang on the way to the mill. It was Raine. I hadn't talked to her all morning, but by now, she'd heard the news. "Hey, Raine, I guess you heard."

"I did. I had three clients, so I haven't had time to call, but Tucker told me all about it. He said you and Emily were the ones to discover them. I'll bet Emily was upset." It was slightly annoying that no one ever considered that I might have been upset about discovering a dead body or, in this case, two. It was true I'd had numerous run-ins with dead people in the past few years, but it would still be nice to hear an occasional "how are you doing?" afterward.

"She was pretty shaken," I said.

"So was Tucker," Raine added. "He's called me a few times to talk about it because he still can't believe it. He's very upset." It seemed there was more purpose to this phone call than to check on Emily. Raine was going out of her way to assure me that Tucker was upset about the murders. Had he put her up to it, or had Raine already calculated that her new boyfriend would be a suspect? "I thought we could make some dinner tonight for the guys. Tucker is really lost. He's out of a job now, and he's not entirely sure what to do next."

"That's right. I forgot that he had a record that kept him from finding a job." As I said it, Jackson looked over with a quizzical brow. I mouthed the name Tucker at him. I'd have to fill him in on that detail, too. He was right. I had found out a lot of information during our excursion to the season opener. Tucker had been grateful that Shawn offered him, a man with a record, a job. Arrogant, abusive employer that he was, at least he was able to look past Tucker's history and give him a chance. "I'm sure we can cook up a nice dinner for the guys." I winked at Jackson. "Meet me at my place at five, and we'll come up with a Sunday dinner."

"Yay. Thanks. I'll let Tucker know. He needs to be around friends tonight. See you then."

Raine hung up.

"We're making dinner for the guys tonight—and you're one of the guys. Tucker is the other."

"What about the record?" Jackson asked.

"It figures the detective zeroed in on that part of the conversation. By the way, Raine went out of her way to tell me how upset Tucker is about the murders."

"Did he put her up to it?"

"That question floated through my head. I'll see if I can bring that up with her in a gentle way so she doesn't think I'm fishing for evidence. Tucker was arrested for theft in his early twenties. He did his time and then found that the record hurt his job opportunities. But Shawn Griswold was willing to look past it and hire the man. That does then beg the question—why would Tucker kill his employers if he was sure he'd struggle to find another job? Is there such thing as an anti-motive, a reason not to kill someone? If there is no word, I think there should be. What do you think?"

"About your new word?"

"No, about Tucker having far less reason to kill his employers than other people."

Jackson turned down the dirt road leading to the mill. Unlike a few hours ago, when it was dotted with official vehicles and a few curious neighbors, it was entirely deserted. Jackson pulled up to the house and parked.

"You're right. It does move him lower on the list. We knew Shawn wasn't a nice person to work for but then he did offer Tucker a job. I know having an arrest record, no matter how far in the past and no matter how trivial the crime, is a red flag for employers."

We got out of the car and headed into the house. The body was gone, but the blob of dough remained. It had flattened out to a soupy mess. Some of the cinnamon sugar had been swept up, and it had been tracked around the kitchen by the many feet that had trampled through.

"Were they able to get any kind of print out of the cinnamon sugar spill?" I asked.

"No, but they picked some up so it could be analyzed for traces of rubber or anything else that might help. They combed through the bedroom and the other rooms for those phones, but like I said, with two crime scenes, the search was probably not as thorough as it could have been."

"I'll need gloves." I held out my hand, and he gave me a

new pair. As I pulled them on something occurred to me. "Hmm, I wonder..." I walked over to the drawers in the homey part of the kitchen and started opening them. I pulled them out one by one. There were cooking implements in one, jars of spices in another and a third was filled with oven mitts. I moved aside a few of the mitts, and there it was, the cell phone. I pulled it out and held it up.

"How on earth?" Jackson asked. He couldn't hide the sparkle of pride in his eyes.

"I'd like to say it was instinct or a sixth sense, like Raine, but whenever Emily is baking something that requires handling a lot of sticky dough"—I motioned toward the flat pool of yeast dough on the counter—"she hides her phone in a drawer. That way if she gets a text or call, she can't answer it. She's done it a few times and forgotten about all the dough on her hands. Took a lot of work to clean the phone. It's a trick she read about online, so I thought maybe Amanda used the same trick." I stared at the phone in my hand. "It's asking for a code."

"Of course. I'll have to take it to the station and let the techies give code cracking a try."

"Unless," I said and punched in six zeros. It opened.

"Sixth sense?" Jackson asked.

I shook my head. "No, I'm embarrassed to admit, she uses the same code as me."

"You mean—"

"Yep. In my defense, my phone opens to face recognition, and it rarely asks for a code."

Jackson moved around me to look over my shoulder as I thumbed through her latest texts. There were a few to friends and acquaintances about the season opener. Her last text to Annie was about how delicious the cider donuts were and how people were looking forward to them.

"Scroll down her list of contacts so we can look specifically at our suspects. Start with Jonah."

I peered over my shoulder at him.

"Yes, I'm still leaning toward Jonah."

I scrolled down and found Jonah's name. I tapped it. The last text said "can you add three onions to the order?" I scrolled up on the page. "She only texted Jonah three times and the onion text was sent months ago, and there was a short 'yes' reply. I didn't get the impression that Amanda was deeply involved in the business and operational side of things."

"I'm sure Jonah dealt mostly with Shawn," Jackson said. "I'll go out and give the mill another look to see if I can track down his phone."

I continued my perusal of Amanda's phone. She'd had a lot more contact with Annie. In fact, she'd called Annie last night, but it only lasted a few seconds. She sent a text afterward asking what degree the hot oil needed to reach for the donuts. Not surprisingly, there was no response from Annie.

Amanda's conversations with Riley, her brother-in-law, had also been few and far between. The last text was about Thanksgiving dinner—last Thanksgiving. They obviously didn't communicate much. I scrolled through to Tucker's name. Again, only a few texts and the last one was sent a week earlier. Amanda was letting Tucker know that she'd purchased the banner for the season opener and that he should hang it the day before so the wind wouldn't ruin it like last year's banner.

There was nothing in any of her texts that seemed out of the ordinary or crucial to her murder. Tracy's name was right above Tucker's. I tapped to open the screen. There weren't many texts, not like I had on my phone with my sisters and Raine. But then Taylor was Shawn's cousin, so maybe there wasn't a big connection. The last two texts were sent last week, and the replies were curt and harsh. "You've got to come clean," Amanda had written. Tracy had replied with "mind your own business." The last text was sent the following day. "You'll get caught and it will be embarrassing." Tracy didn't reply to that message.

I glanced at the cookie jar. The big colorful rooster was smiling back at me. The paper was gone, bagged and labeled by the evidence team.

My phone rang. It was Jackson. "Hey, I found something of interest," I said.

"Me, too. I found the phone on a shelf behind the modern apple press. It was high up, not at eye level, so I guess the team missed it. Your highly secure code of six zeroes doesn't work. Might have to take this one in for the techs. I'll head over to the house, so you can show me what you've found."

"See you soon." I hung up and glanced at the texts again. They might not have had anything to do with Amanda's murder, but something told me the curt texts had plenty to do with Tracy's job as treasurer.

CHAPTER 19

We managed to pull together a dinner of baked chicken and mashed potatoes. Raine had talked nonstop about what a wonderful guy Tucker was and how she was convinced she'd finally found *the one*. Edward listened to our conversation raptly, unusual for him because he normally faded away when Raine was in the house. She had a huge crush on my ghost, but now her affections had turned elsewhere. It was even possible that Edward was slightly jealous. He added in a few scoffs and groans as she went on about how talented Tucker was at fixing things and how chivalrous he was when it came to opening doors and pulling out her chair. It was fun to see Raine so happy and starry-eyed. She'd been looking for someone like Tucker for a long time.

We decided to make some chocolate cupcakes, so there'd be a nice dessert. Tucker was very upset by the tragic turn of events, so Raine was sure the cupcakes would help.

The cupcakes were from a box, but I made the frosting

from scratch with butter, cocoa and powdered sugar. I scraped a little off the side of the bowl for a taste. "Hmm, delicious. Just do not tell my sister that we made the cupcakes from a box."

"Who uses a box to bake cakes?" Edward drawled. He'd secured a viewing position at the end of the kitchen table.

"Not literally from a box. There's a mix inside the box, and we used that to make the cakes," I explained. He looked puzzled so I shook my head. "Never mind."

His focus was pulled to the window. "Someone is here," he said. "Must be this brilliant, talented, chivalrous man you've been waiting for," he said wryly to Raine.

Raine pulled off her apron and smoothed her hands over her hair. "How do I look?" she asked me.

"Overly anxious," Edward answered.

Raine was so smitten with Tucker, she didn't even answer Edward. She ran to the front door.

I turned, holding my frosting spatula in my hand, and grinned at Edward.

"What? It's true. She's over-anxious. A little grace and decorum go a long way."

"You're jealous," I said.

He scoffed loud enough to wake Newman from his nap. The dog was sure it was a signal to play ball. He jumped up from the pillow, snatched his tennis ball and sat dutifully in front of Edward.

I put down the spatula. "No, not now, Newman." I heard their voices in the hallway. Raine was giggling and talking animatedly. Edward might have been right about the over-anxious thing, but I was sure that would all smooth out once they'd dated for a while. "Don't even think about throwing that ball," I whispered to Edward. The gleam in his eye indicated he might just do it. I raced to the pantry and pulled out the dog treat jar, the one thing that could get Newman's attention off his ball. The treat worked, so that crisis was averted.

"Go find someplace else to be," I hissed to Edward just as Raine entered the kitchen.

Tucker came in behind. His hair was combed and greased down, and he was wearing a gray dress shirt that was slightly wrinkled and buttoned to the top. He was carrying a bottle of white wine. He offered it to me with a shy smile. "I'm not great at picking wine, but the woman at the liquor store said this is a popular brand."

"Thank you. Can I get you a glass right now? Jackson texted that he'd be a little late, but dinner will be ready soon."

"I guess he's busy—what with all that's happened," Tucker said.

"Brilliant with words, I see," Edward said from somewhere in the room. Raine looked around to find him, and I gave her a "stop doing that" look. She was still new enough to my very big, very annoying secret that she occasionally forgot only we could hear and see him.

I opened the bottle of wine and poured Tucker a glass. He looked at it with a grimace. I laughed. "I'll bet you're more of a beer guy."

He smiled. I walked to the refrigerator and pulled out a cold beer. "Jackson is a beer guy, too."

Tucker sat at the table with his bottle of beer. "How is it going? Have they caught the madman who did this?"

"Not yet, but rest assured, Jackson will solve this, and soon."

Tucker nodded and took a long swig of beer. My phone rang. It was Jackson. I walked to the hallway to take the call.

"Are you going to be here soon?" I asked. "Dinner is ready."

"Is Tucker there?" he asked.

"Yes, we're just waiting on our fourth dinner mate," I said airily. But I wasn't getting the same airy vibes from his end.

"I'll be there soon," he said and hung up.

I stared at the phone, confused by his brusque manner. Raine was laughing exaggeratedly at something Tucker said. When I got back to the kitchen, Edward stared at me. "I stand by my earlier comments."

I ignored him. "Jackson is on his way, but we can get things started. Raine, why don't you sit? I'll serve the food."

Raine was all too happy to sit with her glass of wine and chat with her boyfriend. I, on the other hand, was anxiously waiting for mine to arrive. My intuition told me something was up, and it wasn't good. I filled four plates with chicken, potatoes and salad. I set Jackson's on the table, anticipating his arrival any second. Only I got a terrible sinking feeling when I heard his car pull up. Maybe I did have that sixth sense, after all.

The dogs greeted Jackson, but he barely paid them any attention. His expression was grim when he walked into the kitchen. My other two guests seemed to realize instantly that something was up.

Jackson nodded to Raine and Tucker. "Tucker

Carmichael, I'm afraid I've got some bad news. We found the gun used to kill the Griswolds. It's registered to you."

Raine's shoulders sank, and her gaze, both worried and incredulous, flashed my direction. I had no response. I knew that forensics was tracing down the gun's owner, but I had no idea it would be traced to Tucker.

"That's impossible," Tucker said. "I only have one, and I keep it in my glove box, in my truck. I only just got my rights to own a gun back last year, and I keep it for protection, that's all."

"Let's go out to your truck right now and have a look," Jackson suggested.

Tucker hopped up. "Of course. You'll see there's been a mistake."

Raine had her arms folded around herself, and she refused to even look my direction. We all made a somber shuffle to the truck. Only Tucker seemed sure that this would go his way. He opened his truck and opened the glove box. He moved a few things around, then climbed into the passenger seat to get a better look inside the box. He pulled everything out— gloves, his registration, a wrench and a map book—but there was no gun.

He scratched the side of his head. "I know it was in here. Someone must have taken it." He shot Jackson a pleading look. "You've got to believe me."

Jackson was standing in what I called his official detective pose. He knew this was anything but a usual arrest, and he, no doubt, felt the daggers Raine was shooting at his back, but he pressed on. "Tucker, where were you this morning between the hours of five and eight?"

Tucker looked rightfully flustered. It was hard not to feel sorry for him. "I was in bed until around seven, then I made myself some eggs and coffee. I live alone. But you both saw me when I got to work. I came straight from my house to the mill, and I can tell you I was stunned by the whole scene."

"I'm sorry to have to do this, Mr. Carmichael, but I'm going to need to take you in for questioning. Your gun was used in a double homicide, and we need to find out how that happened."

"I never lock my truck. So stupid of me." Tucker's hands were shaky as he unbuttoned the top button on his shirt. He'd gotten dressed up for a nice dinner, but it had ended in disaster, and from the chilled waves of anguish I was getting from my good friend, Raine, this night was only going to get worse.

CHAPTER 20

My coffee was getting cold, but I didn't feel like drinking it. I tried for the fifth time to call Raine, but she didn't answer. I couldn't blame her, really, and at the same time, I couldn't blame Jackson. He was doing his job. Besides, if Tucker turned out to be the killer, then Raine would be thanking him. I was still holding out great hope that Jackson got this one wrong. If Tucker had carelessly kept his gun in an unlocked vehicle, then someone else could have stolen it to frame him.

"It seemed your dinner party ended in calamity last night," Edward said with a little too much glee in his tone.

"What is with you, Mr. Spoilsport? You complain that Raine is an utter nuisance, but when she brings someone to the house—someone who has, as you would put it, *caught her fancy*—you were obnoxious and annoying about it."

"I do find her a nuisance. It's just that I didn't get a good feeling about that man."

"No, you were obnoxious long before he walked in," I argued.

"Agreed, although obnoxious is a harsh word. After he entered the house, I thought he seemed wrong or off. Not trustworthy."

"How could you possibly make that judgment in the few minutes he was in the house? I think you don't want to admit that you are fond of Raine."

Edward scoffed. "Believe what you will. I'm going outside." Now that Edward's world had opened up to include the back stoop, he spent a lot of time out there, and that was fine with me.

I drank the cold coffee, wincing at the taste, and grabbed my keys. Hopefully there'd be some tasty treats for Monday's staff meeting. I'd give Raine some time. With any luck, Jackson would clear Tucker of any wrongdoing by lunch.

Myrna, the office manager and woman responsible for just about everything, was setting cheese Danish on a tray when I walked in. She smiled at me over her shoulder. "I saved you one of the almond bear claws you like so much. It's on your desk."

"Boy, it's good to have friends in high places," I said.

Myrna laughed. "Oh, you mean me and my lofty position as pastry arranger?" She finished her task and joined me at my desk with her own pastry, a luscious-looking cherry Danish. "I heard what happened at the cider mill," Myrna said. "Lauren is in with Prudence right now. They're trying to find her a new assignment since her last one ended in murder. I think Prudence will want to shift you over to the murder story."

"Well, darn," I said.

Myrna's penciled in brows danced up. "Really? I thought you preferred those kinds of stories."

"It's true, I do and doesn't that make me a bit odd? But I'm following the financial problems at the Small Business Society. I was sure that would be a dull story, but I think something is going on there. In fact, I was hoping to talk to Prudence about it. I'm sure she has some insider information that will help me figure out what's going on over there."

Parker, the editor—mostly in name—walked in. When I first got hired, Parker was the manager, editor and overall boss of the newspaper. Then Prudence Mortimer bought the paper, and she decided to take a big hand in running the operation. She'd kept Parker on, and he stayed because he was still making the same salary, but his responsibilities had been greatly reduced. I was pretty sure his Mondays consisted mostly of trying to decide which pastry to eat. He muttered his usual "hello" to Myrna and me and then headed straight to the pastries.

Lauren came out of Prudence's office a few minutes later. She was frowning, unusual for her. "I had such a good piece written about the cider mill season opener." She decided to explain her frown before I could ask. "But Aunt Prue says we're not going to run it because of the—well—you know. It makes sense I guess, but I really put my heart and soul into this one, and I got some great photos." She sat down with a plunk at her desk. "Oh my gosh, I'm terrible. Those poor people are dead, and I'm angry that my piece won't be published."

"We've all been there." I got up, hoping to get a word with Prudence before she came out to start the meeting. Her self-important footsteps assured me I was a few seconds too late. Prudence stepped out of her office with her clipboard.

"Please, enjoy the pastries, everyone. They were warm when I bought them. Now, let's see, business to discuss." She picked up her pen and drew it down the paper on her clipboard. "Parker, I'll need two more advertising slots filled. The Griswolds had reserved two spots in the paper, but I think we can assume we won't be getting any copy for those." Prudence glanced across the room at me. "I assume you're on that story, the murder of the cider mill owners?"

"Uh, yes, I guess so. I also wanted to talk to you about my other story—"

Prudence's brows bunched, then smoothed. "Oh right. That one. We'll talk about it in my office. So, Lauren, you're going to do an article about next weekend's pet show, and Myrna, I have those balance sheets you needed. If there's nothing else, Sunni, let's talk in the office."

I headed to Prudence's office. She always had it perfumed with sachets and candles. Today was no different. It took me a few seconds of nose wriggling to work out the kinks caused by the strong scents.

"Close the door, please, Sunni."

I closed the door and sat down in the upholstered chair across from her desk. An entire family of ceramic kittens, complete with little bows, smiled down at me from the shelf above her head.

Prudence folded her hands on her desk and started right in. "I've been contacted by Peter Zander, the president of the society, and he's asked that we step back from our newspaper coverage of the SBS. He'd like to solve any issues without the publicity, and since Mr. Zander is an important local businessman, I think it's best if we kill the story."

I sat forward. It took me a second to find my words because I hadn't expected the ones she'd thrown at me. "I do believe something very scandalous or, at the very least, dishonest is going on with the society's finances. There was a group of people at that meeting, and they are determined to get to the bottom of it, so why not get ahead of the story, break it ourselves?"

"That story will fade behind the big, explosive news of the double murder. Let's focus on the Griswolds' untimely, violent deaths. You've said it yourself—that's the kind of story that sells newspapers."

"So do financial scandals, especially when they involve respected associations like the Small Business Society. Heck, they might even be related." I tossed that zinger out to slow her down. She was obviously determined to squash the SBS story. At the same time, it had been dancing through my head, the notion that the two things were connected.

Prudence sat forward. "Why do you say that?"

I shook my head. "Too early to connect dots. But did you know that Tracy Goodwyn, the SBS treasurer, is Shawn Griswold's cousin?" I immediately regretted the question. Prudence had lived her whole life in Firefly Junction, so of course she knew that detail.

Her expression assured me that was the case. "I don't see how any of that matters. Tracy Goodwyn might be an inferior treasurer, but she's not a killer. Besides, my friend who is married to the chief of police told me they'd already made an arrest, and it's only a matter of time before an official announcement is made. In fact, you should probably hurry down to the precinct so you're there when it happens. And as for the Small Business Society, that will be handled in-house. No need for a story."

"Fine." I got up to leave. I felt deflated. She was obviously more concerned about her good standing in the society than getting to the truth of the matter. That was never a good stance for a newspaper owner, but it was the way she ran things. What had me more distressed now was that there was news of an arrest and imminent charges. I could only assume it was Tucker. Jackson had not called me since he took Tucker in for questioning. Maybe it was time I gave him a call.

CHAPTER 21

I'd been so distraught that Raine was no longer speaking to me, I all but leapt at my phone when I saw her name come up on the screen. "Hi, Raine."

"Hey," she said dejectedly. "Sorry I've been such a boob. I know none of this is your fault, and Jackson is just doing his job. I just wish he'd do it a little less efficiently."

"Would you only tell someone half of what you saw in tarot cards?" I asked.

"No, although occasionally there is stuff that I frost a bit to make the future sound less dire. Anyhow, have you heard anything?"

"No, not yet. But I'm glad you called. I was sitting here at my desk, unabashedly finishing my second bear claw and trying to figure out where to go with this case and something occurred to me. Tucker drives a very noisy truck."

Raine piped up before I could explain. "I hardly think he

needs to hear complaints about his noisy truck. He already gets enough of those from his neighbors."

"Aha, see, that's my point. Growing up, a man named Ernie Belmont lived two doors down, and one day he came home with a very loud motorcycle. Well, Ernie worked the late shift at a local warehouse, so he got home around three in the morning. That motorcycle woke the whole neighborhood. He eventually had no choice except to sell it because the neighbors all but gathered their torches and pitchforks. I felt bad for the man because he really loved that bike. Anyhow, enough about that. I was going to head over to Tucker's house and ask a few neighbors if they heard the truck Sunday morning. It's not anything too profound, but it's a start on my quest to clear Tucker's name. He doesn't seem like a killer."

"Thank you, Sunni. You're the best. I don't think he's a killer either. He looked so upset when Jackson led him away last night. He told me no one ever believes you once you've been arrested of a crime. It's not fair."

"I agree. And he looked genuinely shocked that his gun wasn't in the glove box."

"I'll text you his address. Let me know what you find out, and Sunni, thanks for doing this. Tucker doesn't have money for a good lawyer, so he'll need our help."

"You bet. I'm on this murder story now, so I'm determined to get to the bottom of it."

While the Griswolds lived on the end of town where neighbors were spread far, Tucker Carmichael lived in a neighborhood where the houses sat on small yards and neighbors were so close you could chat with one another through an open window.

Tucker's house was small and boxy with gray siding and white window trim. The driveway in front of a one-car garage was empty. I assumed his truck was still at the precinct. It was being searched for evidence. If that was the case, it meant there was enough reason to keep Tucker overnight. That didn't bode well for my quest to clear his name, but hopefully, this trip to his neighborhood would help.

I parked in front of Tucker's house. It was a quiet street with a few maple trees lending their charm to the landscape. Because the houses were so close and the street was quiet, it didn't take long for a woman in the house next door to pull back a curtain and glance out to check on the unfamiliar Jeep.

I got out and waved, then headed across to her house. She dropped the curtain quickly, and I wondered if I'd scared her. But seconds later her front door opened and she walked out holding a small tan dog. The dog wriggled in her arms, so she set him down on the stoop, and he pounced down the steps to greet me. His tail wagged and he barked up at me. I leaned down to stroke his soft fur.

"Are you looking for someone?" the woman asked. "If you're looking for Tucker, he must be out of town. He didn't come home last night. Not that I'm always watching out the window"—which she clearly was—"but his truck rattles all the dishes in my cabinet."

It was exactly what I wanted to hear.

I patted the dog on the head and straightened.

"Come on, Tiger, get back inside. You've greeted her, now go on. Back inside." The dog understood the command. He took one more circle around my ankles and then trotted inside.

"I was hoping you could answer a question for me," I said.

She smiled. It seemed she liked the idea of providing information and that made my task much easier. "What's this about?"

I showed her my press pass, and that increased her smile tenfold. "I'm Sunni Taylor. And you are?"

"Oh my, from the *Junction Times*. We don't get many reporters on this street. I'm Lisa Ingersol. What's this about?"

I'd been working on a reason to ask my questions without alerting the neighbors to Tucker's latest legal troubles. I was sure it was one of those neighborhoods where rumors spread like wildfire, and once someone was even considered a suspect in a murder, their reputation would take a hit.

"I'm doing an article on noise pollution, and I've heard that someone on this road drives a noisy truck, one that has caused some problems in the neighborhood."

Her smile stayed plastered in place as she nodded along, and her gaze flicked toward Tucker's house. "I'm surprised you've heard about that. News sure does travel in this town. That noisy truck belongs to my neighbor, Tucker." She waved her hand toward his house. "He's a nice enough man, even takes in my trash cans occasionally, but that truck. I know it's all he can afford, and now he'll probably lose his rental house, too."

"How's that?" I asked. I knew where this was heading, but I wanted to hear what Lisa knew about the murders.

Her smile widened, and her eyes brightened, too. "You haven't heard? I would have thought a newspaper reporter would have been the first to know. Someone killed the owners of the apple mill and right during their season opener. Tucker worked for the Griswolds, so now, he'll be out of a job."

"Right. I think I heard something about that. What a shame. Just a few details. Since Tucker didn't come home last night, when was the last time you heard that loud truck start up?"

Admittedly, it was an odd question, but I didn't know how else to phrase it. Fortunately, Lisa was too excited to share information to note that it was a strange question.

She took a few seconds to think about it. "Let's see. I was watching a morning prayer service on television, and I had to turn it up when Tucker started that darn truck. That must have been around nine in the morning."

Relief washed through me. "Nine? Not any earlier?"

"Nope, it was nine."

"So, you didn't hear the truck earlier?"

It was one question too far. Her smile faded, and her brows bunched. "No, that was the first I heard it all morning. What's this about? Is it just about noise pollution?"

"Yes, I'm wondering how often that truck wakes the whole neighborhood. Or maybe it's not that loud," I added.

"Oh, it's that loud, all right. During the week, when he goes to work early, it wakes me right out of a sound sleep. Tiger, too." She chuckled. "The dog thinks that truck is his personal alarm clock. The truck vibrates the house and then Tiger hops to his feet, stretches and starts barking for breakfast. That's how I know I didn't hear that truck before nine. Tiger let me sleep late yesterday morning."

"Well, thanks for your help. I won't keep you any longer."

"Will I get a mention in the paper?" she asked. "On the other hand, come to think of it, I don't want Tucker to know I've been talking about that darn truck."

"I won't mention you then. Thanks again." I practically skipped back to the Jeep. I had something big, and I was sure it would help Tucker's case. I pulled out my phone the second I sat behind the wheel. I was expecting to leave a rambling voicemail but Jackson answered.

"Hey, did Cash get that extra bucket of grain this morning? Edward's right. I think he's too thin."

"Straight to the horse. No 'hello, sunshine, how is the love of my life?'" I teased. "And to answer your question, yes, I gave him the bucket of grain, and he was extremely happy. Now, onto other things. Tucker has a very loud truck, and his neighbor, who insists the truck wakes her out of a sound sleep, did not hear him start the truck until after nine on Sunday morning. She remembers the time because she had to turn up the volume on her televised church service."

"I was going to head over to his house and talk to the neighbors about just that. I released Tucker this morning. He's not off the hook yet," he added briskly. "But so far, all I've got is the gun. He told me he was distraught about no longer having a job, and that he worries he'll lose his rental house. That alone makes it hard to see why he'd kill the Griswolds. However, like I said..."

"Right. He's not in the clear *yet*. I think when you talk to his neighbors he will be. His truck has been a source of contention in his small neighborhood. It's Ernie Belmont all over again."

"Who?" he asked.

"Not important. I've got another call coming through. Such is the life of a busy reporter. I'll talk to you later."

"Yep. Later, Bluebird, sunshine, love of my life."

"Too late." I laughed as I flicked over to the other call. It was Emily.

"Hey, Em."

"Sunni, where are you at?" Emily was whispering into her phone.

I sat up in alarm. "Em, is everything all right?"

"Yes, I'm fine. I've got a visitor." She was still whispering.

"Say 'eggplant' if you're in some kind of trouble."

She laughed quietly. "Eggplant? Really? I'm not in trouble. Annie Blair is here. She's upset. She says she overheard something that might be important, but she's too nervous to go to the police. I told her you'd come here and talk to her and then you'd relay it to Detective Jackson."

"Oh, wonderful, I'm on my way. Don't let her leave."

"I won't. See you soon."

CHAPTER 22

I was glad to see another car still parked at Emily's. I was worried Annie would get cold feet and leave before I could hear what she had to say. As badly as I wanted to stop in the barn and say hello to Arlo and Angel, I willed myself across the yard to the house. Snuggles would have to wait.

Emily and Annie were sitting at the kitchen table sipping tea that had a minty scent. Emily's homemade shortbread was stacked on a plate in the middle of the table. "I made you a cup," Emily said as I stepped into the kitchen.

Annie looked up warily from her cup and gave me an even more prudent smile.

"Annie, you remember my sister, Sunni."

"Yes, hello." Annie was tucked down between hunched shoulders, and she cradled the steaming cup of tea as if it was protecting her from danger. I wasn't exactly an intimidating presence, so I could only assume Annie was worried about relaying what she'd witnessed. Of course, I also had to keep in mind that Annie was on Jackson's suspect list, so all of this might be an act. Maybe she planned to give me a good show and tell to throw Jackson off her trail. He'd mentioned that he was going to see her today. Was she hiding here at Emily's farm to avoid questioning? Or was I letting my imagination run away with me? Could definitely be the latter.

I sat in front of the third cup of tea. "Hi, Annie, how are you doing? I'm sure the Griswolds' deaths have been a shock."

She was still gripping the tea. "It's terrible. I'm having a hard time believing it." Annie sat up straighter and released her death grip on the cup of tea. "I heard a rumor that Tucker Carmichael has been arrested. Is it true?" She shook her head. "Tucker can be kind of gruff, but he's not a killer."

"Why don't you tell my sister what you witnessed last week? She can let Detective Jackson know in case he wants to follow up on it."

Emily pointed to her shortbread (as if her delectable, buttery, sugar-coated chunks needed pointing out). I picked one up, deciding that nibbling a cookie might help lighten the atmosphere and make it seem as if we were merely three women chatting over tea and cookies. Plus, they were still warm, and they were making my mouth water.

"Go ahead, Annie, I'm all ears," I said airily. Some people froze up when they were talking to a reporter or, in this case, a reporter with close connections to a homicide detective. I wanted her to feel at ease because she seemed tense.

I'd started the shortbread rounds. Annie picked one up,

took a bite and went on for a few long seconds about how good it was and how she'd have to learn how to make it that way. Emily knew I was anxious to hear her story, so she made a quick promise to send her the recipe. That satisfied Annie's quest to make delicious shortbread.

Annie demurely set down her shortbread, took a long, dramatic sip of tea and then sighed with satisfaction. "Well, it happened last week." She rolled up her eyes. "Wednesday. No, Thursday. I remember because I'd finalized my cider donut recipe, and I was celebrating with a cup of tea." She lifted her cup as an unnecessary visual. She set the cup back down and, once again, cradled her hands around it. "Amanda had been very busy that day, and at the same time, she seemed distracted. When I asked her how many donuts I should make for the first day of the season opener, she looked at me as if I'd asked her to solve the mysteries of the universe. She finally stuttered out six dozen. Then a car drove up to the house. It was Shawn's cousin, Tracy. Amanda rushed outside to greet her, only it was less of a greeting and more of a confrontation."

"I got the sense that the two women were not friends," I said.

"That was only in the last few months. Before that, Tracy stopped by all the time for lunch, or they'd go shopping together, but that all came to an end in summer. Tracy only came around a few times after that, and that was to see her cousin, Shawn. Amanda and Tracy hardly said two words to each other. I figured they'd had a spat about something and that it would be smoothed over eventually, but that wasn't the case."

"Did you get a sense of what the argument was about last Thursday?" I asked.

Annie shook her head. "I only heard bits of it." Her eyes rounded. "Not that I was eavesdropping, but I'd opened the kitchen windows because the oil in the fryer had gotten too hot, and I needed to clear the air so the smoke alarm didn't go off." She laughed lightly. "Kind of ironic that I nearly burned the kitchen down after all."

"The bits you heard—" I prodded.

"Right. Amanda was holding a piece of paper, and she waved it around as she spoke angrily to Tracy. She told Tracy to make it right or else. Up to that point, Tracy had her arms crossed defensively around herself, but she swung out her hand and snatched the paper from Amanda. She tore it up and threw the shreds at Amanda, then she got in the car and left."

"Where was Shawn during all this?" I asked.

"He'd gone into town for supplies. I don't think he knew anything about it. Then Amanda picked up the pieces of paper. She carried them inside. I needed her to add butter to her grocery list, so I found her in the office. She had the pieces laid out like a jigsaw puzzle, and she was recopying everything from the torn paper onto a new sheet. Then she folded the paper and came into the kitchen for lunch. She stuck the paper under the cookie jar, and I think she forgot all about it. Never saw her take it out or look at it again."

The paper with the number columns—I knew it was important.

Annie finished her tea but declined a refill. "I need to go home and fix Carl lunch. So, what do you think?" Annie turned to me. "Do you think it's something Detective Jackson should know?" She shrank down some. "He called to let me know that he'd stop by my house later, so I could answer some questions about the Griswolds. I'm afraid to tell him what I saw because Tracy will think I was eavesdropping."

"It's important, and he needs to hear it. I can tell him, but it'll be better coming from you," I explained.

"I suppose you're right. I watch enough of those crime shows, I'm sure he'll want to know where I was at the time of the murders." She pressed her hand to her chest. "I can't believe there were two murders and both people I knew well. I guess that's why the detective is dropping by."

"You should be fine as long as you can tell him where you were Sunday morning." I was hoping my comment would prompt her to fill in the blank, and it did just that.

"Sunday morning is pancake morning. Carl expects a nice stack of buckwheat pancakes and warm maple syrup. I get up early, around seven, to start his breakfast. We sat at the table for at least an hour talking about what I would do since I'd lost my job. I don't think we finished breakfast until well after eight."

"Sounds like a tight alibi," I said, "but then, I'm not a detective."

"Are you sure about that?" Emily muttered over the rim of her teacup.

I shot her a wink and turned a smile in Annie's direction. "Thanks so much for confiding in me, Annie. I'm sure Detective Jackson will be interested to hear everything you have to say."

Annie's story was intriguing, and it lined up with the paper under the cookie jar, but I still couldn't help but wonder if Annie was working hard to throw another suspect onto the pile because she had something of her own to hide. It seemed I still had a lot of work to do.

CHAPTER 23

I'd texted Raine that I had good news for Tucker's case, but she hadn't returned my text. She usually had a full schedule on Mondays, which included working for my sister, Lana. Raine helped with flower arrangements, garland making, cutting out decorations and everything that Lana needed for her events. After my chat with Annie, I decided it was time to talk to Tracy. I knew she was a bank manager, and a quick search of the local banks led me to the right branch. It wasn't ideal to talk to someone at work, but sometimes you had to improvise.

I pulled into the bank parking lot. It was almost empty, which was usually the case for banks with everyone doing their banking online. My phone rang before I could get out of the car.

"Hey, Raine."

"Ugh, I finally broke free from my chains to call you back."

"Yes, it was quite the harrowing task, cutting paper fall

leaves on a die-cut machine," Lana called from somewhere in the room.

"Paper cuts, *madam*, paper cuts," Raine yelled back. "Anyhow, what's up? You said you had good news."

"So far, yes. Tucker's neighbor insists he didn't start his very noisy truck until after nine on Sunday. That fits with his alibi that he was home until then. I let Jackson know. He told me Tucker isn't off the hook yet, but he released him because so far all he has is the gun."

"Thank you so much, Sunni. What a relief. I knew he didn't do it."

"Again, he's not off yet, but I think this will help."

"Still, I owe you," Raine said. "Lunch at Layers? Say in a half hour? If I can stay free of the chains," she added wryly.

"Sounds good. I might be a little late, so order me a Paul Newman. I'm in the mood for roast beef on rye."

"Right, see you there."

I put the phone in my pocket and adjusted my press pass. I was still working on my reason for showing up to Tracy's workplace to ask questions. I walked into the bank. There were two young tellers behind the bulletproof glass, chatting while they waited for customers. A woman in a light green coat and skirt walked out from one of the side offices. "Can I help you?"

"Uh, yes, I'm looking for Tracy Goodwyn."

The woman's face smoothed to a frown, and it suddenly occurred to me—something that should have been obvious—Tracy wasn't working today because her cousin had died the day before. "I'm sorry, Miss Goodwyn is out due to a death in the family. We don't expect her back for a few days. Perhaps there's something I can help you with?"

"No, I need to talk to her specifically. Thank you for your time."

The morning had gone perfectly, but this next strand of my investigation had fallen flat. I could always find out where Tracy lived and approach her at home, but something told me she wouldn't take too kindly to the visit, especially after I sat in on the contentious SBS meeting.

I turned the Jeep back toward Layers. It seemed I was going to be early instead of late for my lunch date. I parked and let Raine know I could order the food because I was early. She sent her sandwich choice, and I headed to the restaurant. My luck had improved. Tracy Goodwyn might have been in mourning, but she was having no problem downing a big sandwich and extra-large soda. She was sitting by herself at one of the tables in front of Layers.

I cleared my throat to pull her attention from her lunch. She looked up, lifted her sunglasses to get a better look and then managed an eyeroll before sliding the glasses back down. "It's the reporter. Surely, you've heard the news, so this is absolutely not a good time for you to talk to me about that silly dustup at the SBS meeting. Prudence was supposed to call her dogs off."

I gritted my teeth as I smiled at her. "Very nice analogy, thanks. And I'm sorry about your cousin and his wife. I can see how broken up you are over it." I usually tried to avoid angering my interviewee right off the bat, but she'd asked for it with her rude comment. "And yes, I understand that the Small Business Society is trying to keep any bad publicity under wraps, but I don't think it's me you have to worry about. Those business owners were angry, and something tells me they're not going to let this drop. By the way, I found something interesting in your cousin's house." I'd said too much.

She sat up rigidly and yanked off her sunglasses. "What were you doing snooping around their house? I should let the police know."

I kept my cool. "Uh, I was the person who found your cousin and his wife. I was delivering pies with my sister, and there was no answer at the door, so I walked into the kitchen. That was when I discovered that Amanda had been shot." She flinched as I said it. I wondered if that was because it was bringing back those fatal moments when she'd confronted Amanda with a stolen gun or if she was genuinely distraught about what'd happened. I wasn't getting a good sense either way, but I was still hating her attitude, so I pushed the envelope a little more. Maybe I could get her to blurt out a confession. "I spotted a piece of paper under a cookie jar, pulled it out and took a photo of it in case it was important." She acted disinterested as I scrolled for the photo.

She wriggled her bottom on the bench and lifted her chin. "I think you should leave me alone, or I'll have a chat with your boss, Prudence. I'll let her know you're harassing me."

"I hardly consider this harassment." I stuck my phone in front of her. (Possibly slight harassment.) "Recognize those columns of numbers? They're the same numbers, only there are two very different totals. I think Amanda was onto something. She knew what you were up to."

Normally, my reflexes were quick, but, in my defense, I hadn't considered the cup of soda a weapon. Tracy threw the cup my direction, and ice-cold cola sprayed all over me.

I had to work hard to keep my calm. I glanced at the mess

on my coat and jeans and smiled up at her. "I guess I hit a nerve."

She stood up from the table, grabbed her sandwich and marched away. She was wearing boots instead of high heels. She'd left behind a stack of napkins. I grabbed them and made a futile attempt to wipe away the drips.

"Sunni? What on earth happened?" Raine asked as she reached the eating area.

"Let's just say I might have gone a step too far in my interview just now. Although, she was asking for it." I looked down at my wet clothes. "And, apparently, so was I."

CHAPTER 24

Raine and I made quick work of lunch. I wanted to get home and shower and change. Jackson was pulling up to the house at the same time as me. I would have liked to think he was there to see me, but I was fairly certain he was there to see his horse.

"Hey, cowboy, are you on break? Need some lunch?" I asked.

"I grabbed a bite to eat on my way here. I was just checking on Cash."

"That's what I figured."

He took my hand and pulled me closer, close enough to notice the stains on my clothes. "Did you spill something?"

"Not exactly." I nodded toward the house, and we headed to the door. "I ran into Tracy Goodwyn at Layers, and I asked her about the paper with the columns of numbers." I stopped and looked at him as we stepped inside. "That's right. I haven't told you about my chat with Annie."

"Just got done talking to her," he said. "She told me about the argument she witnessed between Tracy and Amanda."

"Well, that paper with the numbers sure got a big, unfriendly reaction from Tracy."

Edward appeared in the kitchen. "It's a nice day. Your horse should be in pasture and not locked up in the barn."

Jackson raised a brow toward me. "I guess this is what I can expect from now on." He turned to Edward. "He's perfectly content in his nice big stall. We can't leave him out in pasture all day, or he'll overeat. And since neither of us was home—" Jackson shook his head. "Why am I bothering? He'll just find something else to gripe about."

"I'll follow you out to the barn," I said. "I want to hear how the case is going."

Jackson walked out the back door, and the dogs and I followed. I didn't have to look back to know that my ghost had followed, too, only he couldn't go past the stoop. The goats instantly started calling out when they saw me. I walked to their gate and let them out. Soon, there was a whole parade of us following Jackson into the barn. He glanced back, laughed and muttered something about the Pied Piper.

The dogs stayed in the barn for a moment and then trotted off to chase squirrels. The goats immediately started climbing on the stack of hay bales.

"What did you think of Annie's alibi?" I asked.

"The pancake breakfast with her husband? It's never a solid alibi if the only person who can vouch for you is a close family member, but it sounded reasonable enough. I asked her if she knew that Tucker Carmichael kept a gun in his glove box. I expected a confused look. Instead, she told me yes, she knew about it. She said Tucker liked to talk about his shooting skills, and he pulled it out whenever they spotted a snake at the mill. She knew he kept it handy in his glove box."

"So, if Tucker liked to talk about shooting and guns, it's possible more people knew that he kept one in his glove box," I deduced.

"I'd say so." Cash began murmuring a low whinny as soon as he saw Jackson.

"He already knows you," I said. "I guess that's what they call an instant bond."

That notion made Jackson smile. He patted Cash's neck. "I think I'll groom him." He stepped into the stall and put on his halter. A few seconds later he had the horse standing in crossties in the middle of the barn aisle.

He began vigorously brushing Cash's brown coat. "I also talked to several of Tucker's neighbors, and as you mentioned, none of them heard the truck start before nine. Apparently, that noisy truck has become the talk of the neighborhood."

"That's the impression I got." I plucked a hairbrush out of the brush box to comb Cash's mane. The stiff black hair was thick and long, and it made the horse especially beautiful. "I assume that pretty much takes Tucker off the list, right?"

Jackson paused his grooming and looked at me over the horse's rump. "Unless he found a different way to get to the mill. But it seems he didn't leave the neighborhood before nine, so that puts him lower on the list."

I sighed loudly. "Really?"

"Look, I know you want this all to go well for Tucker because he's Raine's boyfriend, but the fact of the matter is that two people were shot with Tucker Carmichael's gun. And we now know something more about him. He's a good shot. You don't take out a snake with a bullet unless you've got good aim."

"Still, you admit this is looking better for him?" I prodded.

"Yes, it is. Now, what happened to you?" he asked.

I glanced up, confused. He reminded me by looking pointedly at the cola stains on my coat.

"Oh right, my run-in with the flying cup of cola. I just happened to run into Tracy Goodwyn at Layers."

Jackson peered over the horse's back. "Just happened to?"

"*Yes*, actually. How on earth would I know what her eating schedule was? Of course, I had stopped by the bank where she works first only to discover that she was out of office due to a death in the family. Oh, that reminds me—" I looked at him expectantly, but he didn't catch on. We were usually more in sync, but there was a fifteen-hundred-pound horse standing between us. "Did you talk to Riley, Shawn's twin brother?"

"I did. He was still not terribly overcome with grief, but he was walking around in a daze. By the way, there'll be a memorial tomorrow afternoon at the mill. I plan to attend. Maybe our killer will be there looking guilty and upset."

"That'd be nice. Did Riley have anything else to say?"

"Not really. He's standing by his alibi that he slept late. Not much of an alibi, unfortunately. And with his brother dead, he now gets ownership of the mill. He said it's pretty heavily mortgaged and not worth much. He also has no plans to run the place."

"That's too bad. Maybe he can find someone to take it on. The townsfolk love that cider mill."

"He's hoping he can sell it to someone interested in continuing the cider tradition and not just some developers. But he insisted that after paying off the loans on the place, he'd be lucky to come out even. So, no big windfall, apparently, which, if true, leaves him with little motive to kill his only surviving family member. Now, am I going to hear about the soda splash, or are you avoiding the topic?"

"Not avoiding it. Just not as interesting for me because I already know what happened." I started absently braiding the horse's mane. "I approached Tracy, and she already had a major bee in her bonnet because she knew I'd been at the SBS meeting and that things had not gone well for her there. She figured I was still trying to get the scoop."

"Which you were," he noted.

"Yes, but that scoop got bigger because now it might have led to murder. I mentioned and then showed her the photo of the mysterious paper under the cookie jar."

It took a second for Jackson to recall what I was talking about. "Oh yeah, that. So that's the paper Annie saw Amanda copying from the paper that Tracy tore up."

"Right. And I think that column of numbers is from an account book or something like that. Amanda must have copied the numbers, then she added them up and saw that the total was way off. She confronted Tracy about the numbers being off and told her she needed to come clean. And I can tell you that photo triggered quite the reaction." I ran my hand down my coat. "As you can see. She marched off after that."

Jackson gave me his fatherly glum smile. "You need to be careful, Sunni. If she is the killer, then she's dangerous. Adding one more body to her count won't make much difference in terms of a life sentence."

"We were standing right in front of Layers. I was perfectly safe." I glanced down at the spots. "My coat, not so much. And with that, I'll leave you to your new best friend while I go put some spot remover on my clothes."

"I'm talking to Tracy next," Jackson called as I left the barn.

I turned and poked my head back in. "If she's armed with an extra-large soda stand a few feet back."

Edward was still on the stoop. "What's he doing in there? Having a conversation with the horse?"

I smiled up at him. "I'll bet Edward Beckett had plenty of conversations with his horses."

His mouth rolled in, and his image wavered in the breeze. "My horses understood every word I said."

"Of course. Jackson's grooming Cash, then I bet he'll walk him out to the pasture." I stopped on the stoop. "I'm sure you can sit on him again, too."

Edward lifted his chin as if that suggestion was beneath him, but I was sure I would look out on the back stoop in the next half hour and spot my very proud housemate sitting on Cash's back.

CHAPTER 25

The late afternoon sun had settled with brilliant determination in a cornflower blue sky. Jackson asked me to lead Cash back to the barn before I left. He knew, too well, that I was going to keep on with my investigation. After all, I had a story to write and, in this case, I had an additional motive. I wanted to clear Tucker's name. Raine hadn't been this happy in a relationship in a long time, and I wanted to make sure it continued.

I returned Cash to his stall, refreshed his water and headed inside to find a paperclip. The kitchen door on the Griswold's old farmhouse had the same old-fashioned doorknob and lock as the one on my back door. It was an easy one to pick with a straight paperclip. I learned the trick after locking myself out of the house on more than one occasion. I planned to take one more look around the Griswold's house in case we'd been overlooking something important.

Edward watched as I rummaged through my junk drawer in the kitchen for that one necessary paperclip.

"Did you enjoy your time on the horse?" I asked. As predicted, Edward had not turned down Jackson's offer to walk Cash to the back stoop.

"Sitting on a horse is one thing; riding is another thing altogether," he said glumly.

I found the clip and pushed it in my pocket. "I'm sorry, Edward. I know that's where your heart lies." There wasn't anything else I could add. I had no way to help him past this obstacle.

"Yes, well, it's ridiculous for me to dwell on things that can't be changed. Where are you off to now?"

"I'm trying to figure out who killed Amanda and Shawn Griswold."

"I thought that was obvious. Didn't Jackson already arrest the man Raine brought to dinner? She needs a lesson on choosing men," he scoffed.

"It wasn't Tucker," I said confidently.

"No?" Edward asked. "What makes you so sure?"

"Circumstances." I waved my hand to show him I was done discussing it. Edward had a biased view of Tucker. Then again, so did I. I had no way to be certain that Tucker was innocent, but my intuition was telling me there was more to the Tracy Goodwyn story, more that would lead back to the murder. "I'll be back soon."

Jackson mentioned there'd be a memorial at the mill tomorrow afternoon, and I fretted that there might be people at the mill getting things ready for the event, but other than a few crows hanging out in the yard, the property was deserted. I parked my Jeep off to the side and near a big maple tree. I didn't want the neighbors to know anyone was at the house.

I walked to the back door, jammed in the paperclip and with a few pokes and twists, the lock turned. I glanced back. The crows were watching me and seemed to be giving me admonishing glares. I stepped inside. I'd already looked through the kitchen area several times. I was more interested in the office.

I didn't have gloves, but I'd brought a linen handkerchief in case I needed to touch something. Jackson wouldn't be pleased if he knew what I was up to, but since Prudence put me on the murder story, I was considering it part of my job. There was an account ledger in the top drawer of the desk. It belonged to the mill. I glanced through it. I was no accountant or bookkeeper, but it seemed Riley was telling the truth. It appeared a lot more money was going out than coming in. I was sure you'd have to sell a lot of cider and apple pies to make a profit. Not that it mattered now. The season had ended long before it really got started.

I flipped through some papers in a file. There was a sticky note pressed to the front of the folder. Someone had written a reminder. "Write three notices." That was all it said. Everything pertained to the mill, and it had nothing to do with the Small Business Society. I was in the wrong office. I needed to look around Tracy Goodwyn's office. I grinned to myself, wondering if she had one of those easy-to-pick locks.

I walked over to the framed photos on the wall of the office. There was a nicely framed wedding photo of the Griswolds. They'd been a handsome couple, and Amanda looked radiant in her white gown and veil. Shawn's brother was in the next photo. The three of them were standing in front of a giant redwood. Riley was using a cane, and he didn't look as happy as the couple next to him. There was an old black-and-white wedding photo of a couple I was certain were Riley and Shawn's parents and then a few more of the Griswolds standing in front of the mill. As I perused the photos, the kitchen door opened. I sucked in a breath and held it as I glanced around for a hiding place. There was a closet door on the other side of the room.

I tiptoed across and slipped inside. It was filled with skis and winter parkas. I tucked myself in and left the door slightly open, so I could spy on the apparent intruder. Maybe it was the killer coming back to the scene of the crime.

I stood as still as I could. It wasn't easy surrounded by winter gear, but I managed. I peered through the slit left by the open door and realized I wouldn't see much unless the intruder stepped deep into the office, specifically to the desk. I was in luck…at least for someone hiding in a closet. Footsteps creaked the office floor and a figure appeared. I nearly groaned in disappointment. It was Tucker.

I stayed perfectly still and watched as he rummaged through the desk drawers. He seemed to be looking for something, and I badly wanted to know what. I stayed silently tucked inside my hiding spot, but as I shifted my weight, the floor beneath me creaked. Tucker's face popped up, and he looked in the direction of the closet. I froze like a statue. Tucker seemed to decide it was just the usual settling of an old house. He went back to searching through the desk.

My journalist's curiosity got the best of me. From my vantage point, I could see that he was unarmed. Besides, his gun was still at the police station. If he made a move to attack me, I was a very fast runner. That was all I needed to coax myself out of the closet. I pushed the door open slowly. Another creak followed and Tucker's head snapped up. His eyes were round, and he was backing up, ready to make a run for it. He saw me, and his chin dropped.

"Sunni, what are you doing here?"

"I was searching for more clues about the murder. I shouldn't be here, but I was hoping to find something that would help clear *your* name."

The creases smoothed from his forehead. "That's very kind of you," he said.

"I'm doing it for Raine. Only I think my plan backfired because here you are snooping around Shawn's desk."

His face blushed pink. "Yeah, you caught me in the act, I'm afraid. But it's not what you think. Please, let me explain."

I nodded. "Go ahead."

"Whenever we did special weekend events like the season opener, Shawn paid me in cash, so I could avoid taxes. I know that's a crime in itself, but it was a nice little bonus."

"You didn't get your pay," I said.

His face dropped. "I'm going to need that money. I'm already out of a job." It was hard not to feel sorry for the man. "I was hoping I'd find the money in the desk." He finally lifted his gaze to me. "Please, please don't tell anyone I was here. I didn't find the money, and so that's that. I won't get paid for Saturday. And please don't mention this to Raine."

"I won't say anything to Raine." I gave it some thought. "I suppose since I'm also inside the house, it seems we both have a secret to keep." His excuse seemed honest and legitimate. He desperately needed that money, and there was no way to get it without entering the house and looking for it. I briefly considered helping him look, then decided that might be pushing it. "I guess we should go."

Tucker nodded. "I guess so. I was surprised to find the back door unlocked. I was sure I was going to have to try all the windows."

This time it was my turn to blush. "I might have coaxed open the lock with a paperclip."

He chuckled. "Don't worry. My lips are sealed."

I peered through the kitchen window to make sure the coast was clear, then we walked out of the house. "I see your truck is out on the street. I guess that's why I didn't hear you drive up," I said.

"And your Jeep is parked behind that tree, so I didn't notice it. I think we both just finished our careers as trespassers."

"I guess so."

Tucker looked at me, his expression filled with gratitude. "Thank you so much for keeping this between us."

I nodded. "Same here." Tucker headed down the long gravel drive to the road, and I climbed into the Jeep. I watched him get into the truck. This was probably something that I should tell Jackson, but for now, I was going to keep it to myself.

CHAPTER 26

It was rare for Prudence to call me personally. She usually asked Myrna to call me and relay messages. I wasn't sure if she felt it beneath her to call subordinates, or she was just generally opposed to making phone calls, but when her name popped up on my screen, I picked it up quickly.

"Hello? Prudence?" I asked in case someone had confiscated her phone.

"Hello, Sunni, yes it's me." She was using her official tone, the one she liked to use at our staff meetings. "I was hoping you could stop in at the newsroom today. I have some news, and I was hoping for an update on the murder case."

"An update? Yes, right." I hadn't left the mill yet, so it would be easy enough to stop by the newsroom on my way through town. "I can be there in ten minutes."

"Great. See you then." She hung up without saying goodbye, but then that wasn't terribly surprising.

I drove back through town. My trip to the mill had gone from mostly uninspiring to shocking to interesting all in a few minutes time. I'd gone through Tucker's excuse in my mind, and there was no reason to think he'd made it up. It made sense. He'd been expecting some cash for the weekend, and it sounded as if he was counting on it. There wouldn't be any other way to collect it.

A good breeze ruffled through the trees and showered my Jeep with colorful leaves as I drove through town. I parked in front of the newspaper office. Myrna's car was no longer parked out front, and I didn't see Parker's either. It seemed it was just going to be me and the boss. I wondered what her news could be. Another reminder not to meddle in the SBS money problem? That ship had already sailed, but she didn't need to know that.

As I got out of the car, it occurred to me that Tracy probably made good on her threat to let Prudence know I'd been harassing her. If that was the case, then I needed to be ready to explain myself. It seemed easy enough, and I had photographic proof that something was up with the SBS books.

I stepped into the newsroom. Prudence was walking out of the breakroom with a cup of tea. "Would you like a cup? It's cinnamon apple."

"No, I'm fine thanks. Where's Myrna?"

"Poor thing had a terrible headache. She looked miserable, so I told her to go home and rest."

"Oh, that's too bad. I'll text her later to make sure she's all right. And Parker?"

"He had to take one of his children to the dentist." She rolled her eyes because Parker was constantly leaving early for this and that. It was somewhat Prudence's fault. She micromanaged the newspaper so much, Parker didn't have enough to do.

"Lauren is out on assignment, so it's just the two of us, which is good. I have some important news, and it's not for public knowledge yet."

I followed her into the office. My nose adjusted to the myriad of perfumy scents, made only more intense by the addition of her cinnamon tea.

I sat in the chair across from her desk. My curiosity was in overdrive.

Prudence took her time getting settled behind her desk, adjusting a few things unnecessarily and taking another sip of her tea. "Hmm, very tasty. It's just what I need in the late afternoon to revive my energy. Are you sure you don't want a cup?"

"Really, I'm fine."

She rested back in her chair. "I've had word from Peter Zander, the president of the Small Business Society, that Tracy Goodwyn has turned herself in."

I sat forward so fast, I nearly slipped off the seat. "She confessed?" I was relieved the case had been solved, and Tucker was off the hook. Raine would be so pleased.

"Yes, it turned out she was, as they say, cooking the books. She was stealing from the SBS. I guess that would explain all those high-dollar shoes and purses." A slightly catty grin followed.

"So, she confessed to stealing from the society? That's all?"

Prudence's lips pursed. "Yes. That's all. What else were you expecting?" It seemed she'd found the answer to her question without me responding. "Oh, you thought she confessed to killing Shawn and Amanda Griswold."

"Yes, after all, that's the case I'm working on," I reminded her.

"Of course." She looked up slyly. "Although I hear you had something to do with prompting this confession. She told Zander that she had no choice because a reporter on the *Junction Times* had photo evidence of the crime."

I shrugged. "It's not anything too incriminating. However, when I showed it to her, she did proceed to douse me with her cup of soda. Why do you think I had something to do with this confession?"

"Zander called me personally to thank me for getting to the heart of the matter through investigation," Prudence said. "Of course, I told him it was my reporter's hard work and not mine."

"Thank you, Prudence."

"He also reminded me in that personal call that he wanted this whole debacle to stay out of the paper."

I nodded. "Ah, I see. The call wasn't just to thank you; it was to make sure none of their dirty laundry was aired. That's fine. I'm onto bigger things now with the murder."

Prudence sat forward with interest. "Right, so how is that going?" She picked up her tea and blew on it, though I was sure it had cooled considerably. Prudence was one of those high-society, pinky-lifted-in-the-air tea drinkers, and that always required a discreet blow.

"I'll be honest, Tracy was my top suspect."

"I suppose you can take her off the list," Prudence said.

"Can I? I'm not so sure. Just because she confessed to one

crime doesn't mean she didn't kill the Griswolds. More than ever, I think she had motive. Amanda knew what she was doing, and I'm certain she confronted Tracy about it. Tracy might have feared that her reputation would be destroyed, and she'd face legal problems, so she panicked and killed Amanda. Shawn was just collateral damage. I'm sure Tracy figured that Shawn knew about her stealing money from the society, too. It seems like something a wife might share with her husband, especially if his cousin was doing the stealing."

"But why would she turn herself in?" Prudence asked.

"To throw the investigation a curveball. She probably calculated that stealing a little money from the society's coffers would only come with a small penalty and possibly a short stint in jail, but a double murder would mean life behind bars. Maybe she thought she'd clear herself of the murder by erasing her motive."

Prudence sat back with an impressed grin. "I hadn't looked at it that way, but what you say makes sense. However, let's give her the benefit of the doubt for now and say she only did the first, much less violent crime. Who else is on the list? There was rumor that the maintenance man for the mill was arrested because his gun was used."

"That's true. However, I've uncovered a few details that don't match up to him being the killer. There is still the baker, Annie Blair. Shawn fired her on Saturday, and she was quite distraught. However, she doesn't seem like the type to shoot two people dead in cold blood."

"You never know. Sometimes people have a much darker side. It's like the moon and the side you can't see," Prudence said.

"That's true. Shawn also fired his produce man Jonah Dowd. Jonah has a hole in his alibi that happens to line up with the time of the murders. So, he's still on the list. And Shawn Griswold has a twin brother, Riley. He doesn't have much of an alibi, but he does stand to inherit the mill."

Prudence's brows arched up in interest.

"Unfortunately, it seems the mill is heavily in debt, so there won't be much to inherit."

"And Shawn's brother knew this?"

"He did. He said he'll be lucky to break even if he can sell the place."

Prudence frowned. "What a shame that the town might be losing their cider mill for good."

I grinned. "Maybe you should get in the cider making business, too."

Prudence laughed. "I don't know the first thing about making cider."

I could have responded letting her know she hadn't known the first thing about running a newspaper either, but I decided to keep that comment to myself.

Prudence took another sip of tea and smiled. "Well, keep me posted." It was her way of dismissing me. I guessed the conversation was over. I nodded and left the office.

CHAPTER 27

"I'll be late," Jackson texted. "Can you make sure Cash gets that extra bucket of grain, please?"

I smiled at the text. "Already took care of your new bestie."

"You're still my number one bestie," He added a heart emoji.

I pulled the sliced cheese and butter out of the refrigerator to make a grilled cheese sandwich for dinner. I had my paper and pen out to make a quick chart for the investigation. I'd written down the names of my suspects: Annie, Jonah, Tucker, Riley and, of course, Tracy. I had no intention of crossing her off the list. As far as I was concerned, she had big motive, and she was obviously already living a life of crime. It took bad character and a warped conscience to steal from a club that put you in charge of their money because they trusted you with the task. I supposed the lure of two-thousand-dollar handbags and high heels was too much.

LONDON LOVETT

"Looks like you have a visitor," Edward said as he peered out the front window.

I didn't need to see who it was because the dogs let me know. They knew the sound of Raine's car, and they knew treats were on their way. They both tore off to the front door in excitement.

I snatched the paper with the suspect names off the table and shoved it in a kitchen drawer. I didn't want Raine to see Tucker's name on my suspect chart. He was low on the list, but as Jackson had said, he wasn't in the clear yet. The biggest piece of evidence, the murder weapon, still pointed to Tucker.

After a few minutes of treats and pats, we managed to move from the entry to the kitchen. "I was just about to make myself a grilled cheese if that interests you."

"I'm sorry to interrupt your dinner, but yes, I'd take one if you have enough."

I sensed instantly that Raine was feeling down.

"I've got plenty." We reached the kitchen. Raine smiled weakly at Edward and then plunked down at the kitchen table.

"Uh-oh," I said, "that is not a happy, smiley face." I buttered the bread.

Raine sighed dramatically. "I consider myself to be a smart woman," Raine started.

"Well, good for you," Edward said, unhelpfully.

Raine ignored the barb. She was already used to Edward's droll wit. "But when it comes to men," she continued, "I'm the biggest, boneheaded dimwit on the planet." She looked wearily up at Edward. "Please don't bother. I'm already beating myself up about this as it is."

"So, this has something to do with Tucker." I placed cheese

slices on the bread and put a skillet on the stove. "Hold on. I think this conversation requires two glasses of iced tea, freshly brewed." I pulled the tea out of the refrigerator, filled two glasses with ice and poured the tea.

Raine took the glass. "Thanks. I need this." She took a few sips while I dropped the sandwiches into the skillet.

I sat down across from her. "What's going on?" My ears were perked. Had Tucker done something that would change our opinions of him?

"He never has money. I'm mean *never*. Whenever we go out to dinner or a movie, he uses the excuse that he forgot his wallet or that Shawn hadn't paid him yet, then I have to pay. I'm such a sucker. I've been going along with it."

Edward cleared his throat as if we could forget a six-foot-plus ghost was standing in the kitchen. "I believe I mentioned there was something untrustworthy about the man."

I waved at him. "Yeah, yeah, we'll get you a medal later." I got up to flip the sandwiches. "Have you spoken to Tucker about this? Maybe you just need to clear the air about it."

"Well, the reality that I'd been a numbskull jumped up and slapped me in the face."

Edward's image shot forward. "The man slapped you?" he asked angrily.

Raine smiled up at him. Some of those stars had returned. "It's just a figure of speech. Tucker didn't slap me. I came to the stunning conclusion that I was a fool. But thank you for being angry about it," she added with a wink.

"I was merely—" he started and then turned back to the window before disappearing altogether.

Raine looked at me with a questioning brow.

"I think Edward was jealous," I whispered.

"That's preposterous," he yelled back from somewhere in the room.

"Tonight, Tucker and I were supposed to go to dinner," Raine continued. "He told me he was taking me to a fancy restaurant and that he was paying for the whole thing. He said it was his way of letting me know how much I meant to him." Raine glanced down at her clothes. "I put on my best skirt and shoes, and I waited, like a silly girl expecting her prom date. Ten minutes after he was supposed to pick me up, he called and said he couldn't buy me dinner after all."

I knew the reason for that, but I was going to have to soften the edges. "Maybe it's because Shawn couldn't pay him. This weekend ended rather abruptly," I reminded her. "He was probably expecting to be paid for a long weekend of work."

"That's true but I don't know—I think I have to face the fact that he's always going to be penniless. Now it'll be worse for him because he's out of a job. I really like him, but I don't know—I think I'm going to break it off."

"Really?" I asked, slightly stunned. "I'm sorry to hear that, Raine. I know you had high hopes for this relationship." I set the sandwiches on the table and sat down. "You're sure about this? I mean he only just lost his job. Maybe he'll get lucky and find something better soon." I had no idea why I was stepping into this. If she wanted to break it off, it was probably for the best. But she'd seemed very happy with Tucker. She was definitely not happy now. She wore a pout as she picked at her sandwich.

"No, I've made up my mind. I'm going to break up with

Tucker. I hate to kick him when he's down, but better to do it now, before we've wasted too much time together."

"I support whatever decision you make." It was the best I could do. I hadn't expected to be having this conversation with Raine tonight.

We talked of other things and finished our sandwiches and then Raine left to make her difficult call to Tucker.

"She's doing the right thing," Edward said after Raine had driven off.

"Do I hear a touch of jealousy in there somewhere?" I pulled my suspect chart and pen out of the drawer.

"That is utter nonsense. There is something not right about that man, and Raine is far better off without him. And that is the end to this inane conversation. I will leave you to your drawings."

"Not a drawing," I called into the air. "It's a suspect chart," I added. I sat down with a poised pen and stared at each name. Annie had motive. Shawn had fired her on the spot, something that would make anyone feel angry and humiliated. Her alibi of making pancakes with her husband was flimsy at best, and she knew that Tucker kept a gun in his glove box.

Jonah Dowd, who, from the start, seemed to be Jackson's main suspect, had also been fired on the spot. Shawn had really been on a roll that day. He'd left a lot of people angry. Jonah had trouble with the law in the past, and he seemed to have a temper. He also had a hole in his alibi for the morning, a hole that fit in perfectly with the time of murder. It was hard to know if he had any clue about the gun in Tucker's truck, but Annie mentioned that Tucker talked about his gun and shooting skills a lot. It was possible Jonah overheard him bragging about it.

Tracy Goodwyn had good motive. And now, in an odd, impulsive move, she'd decided to come clean about stealing from the SBS. Was she trying to rid herself of the scent of murder? According to Annie, before Tracy and Amanda had a falling out, Tracy was a frequent visitor to the mill. She could have known about Tucker's gun, too.

And lastly was Riley Griswold. If the mill wasn't worth much money, then he didn't have motive to kill his only family. However, he had no real alibi other than sleeping late. He, too, might have known about Tucker's gun. One thing about him stood out. He wasn't terribly grief-stricken about losing his twin brother and sister-in-law. He was shocked yes, but that seemed to be where the emotion ended. Tucker had mentioned that the brothers weren't close. Maybe there was more to their relationship, something that had put them at odds.

I stifled a yawn and put the pen down. I was done thinking about murder tonight. A nice hot bubble bath was calling me.

CHAPTER 28

Jackson was out early with the horse. I made scrambled eggs while he finished with barn chores, chores that he loved doing. The back door opened, and Jackson and the dogs came bounding inside.

"Yesterday, when you walked him in from the pasture, I noticed he was slightly off on the right front," Edward said before I could so much as smile Jackson's direction.

"Good eye." Jackson took off his boots and left them at the door. "I found a small rock when I picked his feet this morning."

"Ah, then I haven't lost my touch," Edward said proudly. Even if he couldn't actually ride Cash, the horse had given him something to think about other than the fact that he was stuck here for eternity. And he really did have amazing intuition when it came to horses.

Jackson washed his hands and sat down to his plate of

eggs. "I got a call while I was in the barn. A possible homicide in Smithville. I'll head over there after I eat."

I sat down at the table. Jackson and I had had little time to talk about the case. "Prudence told me that Tracy Goodwyn turned herself in for stealing from the Small Business Society."

"I heard something about that. But she didn't confess to murder."

"I know. I'm just wondering if she turned herself in to take the suspicion off her for the murders."

Jackson nodded as he chewed his toast. "That's possible. Or she knew that a certain reporter was onto her scheme, so she decided to get a jump on it."

"Yes, that's possible, too." Yesterday, I'd convinced myself that I didn't need to mention Tucker being in the Griswold house, but now that Raine had broken it off with the man, I decided to let Jackson know, in case it was important. First, I had to blurt out my own confession, otherwise none of it would make sense.

"I went back to the Griswold property and went in the house," I said.

Jackson looked up from his eggs. "You did?"

I smiled. "Guilty, and I—well—let's just say I let myself into the house."

"You let yourself in?"

"I did. I didn't find much," I forged ahead. "But while I was there, Tucker Carmichael walked in."

Jackson put down his fork and wiped his mouth with his napkin. "So, both of you were trespassing, and he might be a cold-blooded killer."

"I suppose that's one way to look at it."

"Pretty much the only way in my book."

"Right, well, maybe you need a bigger book. Now, should I continue, or are we just going to engage in useless banter?"

"Go ahead, I'm listening."

"Tucker didn't know I was there. I was—well—not important. He started searching through Shawn's desk. I confronted him."

"Of course, you did. Again, Sunni, his gun was used in the murders."

"I know, and I also knew that his weapon was safe and secure in the station's evidence room."

"Right, because he couldn't possibly own two."

I waved my hand. "Never mind. I'm sorry I started this."

"No, you're right. I'm just angry that I've been called off to another possible murder when I haven't made an arrest in this one. So, he was searching through the desk?"

"Yes, he had a good excuse. He was looking for the cash Shawn owed him for working the season opener. He said he badly needed it, and after talking to Raine, it seems he was telling the truth. What do you think?"

"That does sound like a legitimate excuse. Hopefully, I won't be tied up too long in Smithville. Then I can talk to all the suspects again. It should be cut and dry since we found the murder weapon, but I can't find anything else to connect Tucker to the crime. And he's out of a job now, so his case lacks motive." Jackson finished his plate and put his dish in the sink. "Thanks for the eggs. I need to get going." He walked past me, kissed me on the forehead and headed out.

"Well, darn," I said to myself.

"What's that?" Edward asked.

"Just wondering when Jax and I became my parents. Dad rushing through breakfast and pecking Mom on the forehead before rushing out. I guess I'll need to do something to rekindle some sparks."

"Don't need to hear anything about your rekindling of sparks," Edward said.

I started to clean up breakfast. I was a little lost on my story. There didn't seem to be a clear path to the killer. I hoped that the memorial service at the mill would push me toward some better conclusions.

"Who is this?" Edward was at the window. "Oh, it's him," he said dryly. "The killer."

I hurried to the window. Tucker was wearing a trucker's cap and a frown. "I wonder if he's here to talk about Raine." I groaned and walked to the door.

Edward was in the entry before I arrived. He shrugged. "I'm not leaving you alone with a killer."

I sighed loudly and forced a smile before opening the door. "Tucker, nice to see you. Is anything wrong?"

He pulled off his cap and fidgeted with it as he forced a grin. "Raine broke it off with me."

"Oh, I'm sorry to hear that, Tucker."

He kicked at some invisible dirt. "Can't blame her. She's too good for a loser like me."

The last thing I wanted to do was comfort Raine's ex-boyfriend, but it seemed I'd somehow managed to get myself tangled up in it.

"Please, come in. I'll make you a cup of coffee."

Edward was in the kitchen by the time we reached it. He

had his transparent arms crossed and a fatherly scowl on his face.

"Have a seat. Do you take cream or sugar?"

"Black, please. And thank you. I wasn't in the mood to brew myself a pot this morning. I don't know what happened. I suppose it's because I never have money."

I poured him a cup of coffee and sat down across from him. "Raine is a very busy woman with her business. I'm sure she just realized she didn't have time for a relationship."

"No, I think it's the money," he said confidently. I decided not to debate it, especially because he was spot on with his assessment.

He sipped some coffee and lowered the cup to the table. "Didn't expect it to hit me so hard. I guess I thought we had something. Now I know how Riley Griswold felt. Heartbreak can really kick you in the seat when you least expect it."

I perked up with interest. "Riley Griswold? Did he have his heart broken recently?"

"Not recently, no." He took another sip of coffee. I needed to stop giving people beverages. "Good cup of joe. I think I might have mentioned it, but I went to school with the Griswold brothers. I was mostly friends with Riley. Shawn wasn't an easy guy to like. Riley was much more fun. He dated Amanda Tuttle in high school. You knew her as Amanda Griswold." He dropped his face and shook his head. "May she rest in peace. I hear there's a memorial this afternoon at the mill. They've asked me to set up some chairs."

"Yes, I plan to be there," I said briskly. "So, Riley dated Amanda first?"

"That's right. They were a cute, popular couple, and

everyone was sure they'd marry after graduation. I think Riley thought so, too."

"What happened? Did she turn her affections to Shawn?"

"Sure did, but not until Riley was enlisted and stationed overseas. Poor guy came back badly injured only to find that his sweetheart had gotten engaged to his twin brother."

Bingo. There was motive. It was far enough in the past to make it less than perfect, but it was still motive. It had betrayal, heartbreak and crime of passion written all over it.

"Do you think you could talk to her?" Tucker asked.

"Who? Oh, right, Raine." The Riley heartbreak story had left me spinning with new possibilities, and I'd forgotten the real reason for his visit. I smiled sympathetically at Tucker. "I'm sorry, Tucker, but we're not teenagers anymore. Raine is a grown woman, and she makes up her own mind. I'm there only as a supportive friend. Still, maybe she'll change her mind and decide breaking up was a mistake. In the meantime, try to focus on other things."

He finished his coffee. I didn't have time to sit for long, so I got up to make the first move to the door. Tucker got up reluctantly. "Guess it's for the best," he said sadly. "I've been alone all this time. I'm better off by myself."

I felt bad for the man and felt even worse that I was hurrying him out the door, but I had a murder to solve, and Tucker had just given me a detail that shed new light on all of it.

CHAPTER 29

A gloomy sky of ash-gray clouds cast their shadow over the somber event at the mill. A long table had been set with trays of cookies and apple juice, and another table held photos of Shawn and Amanda Griswold. I recognized some from the wall of Shawn's office. Flower bouquets were piling up next to the table. Apple-scented candles were lit and ready to be handed to each mourner. Annie was arranging more cookies on a tray, and Tucker was moving some of the chairs closer to a small platform that had a microphone and a speaker. Riley had a group of people around him. He wore a grim expression as he nodded politely at their offers of condolence. The crowd was impressive, but there was no sign of Jonah Dowd or Tracy Goodwyn. Jonah wasn't coy about the fact that he didn't care for Shawn Griswold, and Tracy had problems of her own. I could only assume word of the SBS scandal had gotten out, and she probably didn't want to show up at a large social gathering.

There was a book for people to write messages about the deceased couple. I browsed through it, but nothing stood out as significant. I badly wanted to talk to Riley but realized I wasn't going to have a chance. He was the only family member at the memorial, so it stood to reason everyone wanted a chance to talk to him.

"Sunni? Sunni Taylor?" a voice called. It was Annie. She was with a young woman who had short black hair and a butterfly tattoo on her neck.

"Annie, hello."

"Hello, Sunni, did your sister come?" Annie looked around.

"Emily had the vet coming out to give shots today. So, harrowing day at the farm, I'm afraid." I smiled at her young companion.

"Sunni, this is Danielle. She was running the cider stand at the season opener."

"Nice to meet you."

Annie took a peek around and then motioned toward a quiet corner of the yard. "Danielle saw something on Saturday that might be important."

I readily followed them to the far corner of the yard, away from the rest of the crowd.

"I wasn't sure if what she saw was important, but I thought you should hear it," Annie explained.

"Yes, please, go ahead," I prodded.

Danielle was chewing a wad of gum as she spoke. "So, I was taking a break late in the afternoon." Her jaw moved a few times as she chewed the gum. "This was after Annie set the kitchen on fire."

Annie clucked her tongue. "I did not set the kitchen on fire. Tell her the important part."

Danielle nodded. "Right, well, I took a little break and walked around the yard. I was trying to get in my steps." She pointed to her pedometer watch. "My friend and I are in a competition, and I wasn't getting enough steps handing out cider." She moved the gum from one side of her jaw to the other, and it was making my own jaw tired watching her gnaw on the wad. "I was near the rear of the property by the old stone storage shed, and I heard someone giggling." Danielle blushed a little. "I knew it was someone doing something—you know—flirty. Well, I didn't want them to think I was spying on them, so I hid around the corner."

"Sounds like spying to me." Annie grinned. She looked satisfied that she'd gotten a dig in after Danielle's comment about the kitchen fire.

"Nah, I'd never do that," Danielle said plainly. She had that same impenetrable level of confidence as Lauren. "They came out from behind the storage shed. It was Amanda Griswold and a man. At first, I thought it was Shawn, and I thought, 'how cute—they took a few minutes out of their busy day to flirt.' My parents still do that, and I think it's cool." Her comment reminded me of my new quest to rekindle some sparks in my own relationship. "Then he took a step, a bad step, and I realized it was Riley, Mr. Griswold's twin brother. He reached for her hand, but she pulled it away. She said something like 'you know it can never be,' then she ran off looking distraught. Riley looked heartbroken. He kicked the side of the shed with his bad leg, then he winced and leaned down to rub the leg." She took a few more gnaws on the gum. "Then I continued my walk."

Annie looked at me expectantly. "What do you think? Is it important?"

"It might be." I was sure it was, but I didn't want to start rumors, especially at the memorial.

"I've heard that Riley used to date Amanda," Annie added. "Tucker told me."

I nodded. "Yes, I heard something about that."

"Maybe it was a crime of passion," Annie said excitedly. "You know—broken hearts, love triangle, all that good stuff."

Danielle laughed. "Annie, you watch too many crime shows."

Annie's cheeks rounded. "Guilty as charged."

"We should probably get back to the service. It looks like Riley is about to say a few words," I said.

"And they're handing out the lighted candles," Danielle said.

We walked back to the center of activity and picked up our candles. The scent of waxy, artificial apple filled the air. Some people sat down, but I stayed back with those who remained standing. It wasn't too hard for Tucker to spot me in the group. He made his way over to me.

Tucker had pulled on a black sweater, and he had his hair combed and gelled. "I thought Raine might be with you," he muttered as Riley checked the microphone.

"I think she had a busy work schedule," I said. It was the truth, and it also reinforced my earlier comment about Raine being too busy for a relationship.

"That's a shame. I was hoping to see her," Tucker said.

I hoped he wasn't going to be the type to keep bothering Raine about the breakup. It was the last thing she needed.

Riley rubbed his bad leg absently as he cleared his throat and stood at the microphone. "Thank you to everyone who came today to remember my brother, Shawn and my sister-in-law"—he paused, closed his eyes and took a deep breath—"my sister-in-law, Amanda."

While he hadn't shown a great amount of grief, the man standing behind the microphone looked as if he'd gone through something terrible. There were dark rings under his eyes, and his hair was messy. His shirt had a few wrinkles, and his shoulders drooped as he spoke.

I heard some people murmuring behind me, and I tilted my head their direction to see if they were talking about Riley's past relationship with Amanda. His dramatic pause made it seem that he was mourning Amanda's loss far more than his brother's. I dipped my head farther to pick up a few words and discovered, not unsurprisingly, they were talking about Shawn's cousin, Tracy, and the scandal at the Small Business Society. If not for the double murder, I could have been hot on the trail of that scandal and breaking it wide open in my next article. But now everyone knew about it, so the prospect of a sensational headline had passed.

"I think Amanda and Shawn would smile if they saw how many people came here this afternoon to pay their respects," Riley said. "I'll miss them both." His voice wavered. "There are a couple other people who wanted to say a few words. And please don't forget to eat some cookies."

I moved casually around the crowd, admittedly listening in on conversations, but most of the talk was about the money scandal. Tracy wasn't at the memorial, but she'd managed to overshadow the event anyhow.

CHAPTER 30

I waited through all the eulogies, the extinguishing of candles and the hugs goodbye. I wanted to speak with Riley once the crowd died down. I found the perfect opportunity when I spotted him collecting up the flowers to deposit in a large box. Tucker was folding and stacking chairs. He hadn't spoken to me since he asked about Raine.

Riley really did have a profound limp, and his expression was somber as he collected the bouquets.

"Can I help you with that?" I asked.

Riley looked up. "Oh, yes, kind of you. I wasn't expecting so many."

"It's a testament to how well they were loved and respected in this community. It was a lovely memorial service." I scooped up a few bouquets. "How are you doing?"

"I feel as if I just landed on a deserted island. I'm alone."

Riley smiled weakly as we carried the bouquets to the box. "My brother and I had our moments, but I'll miss him. We've been a part of each other's lives since the womb, after all."

"I've always heard that the connection between twins, especially identical twins, was strong. Growing up, Mindy and Macy, a pair of identical twins, lived in my neighborhood. If one of them got hurt, you could see their pain in their twin's face."

Riley was nodding along with that. "Yes, that's true. Shawn and I always knew if something was wrong with the other. When I got hurt on the battlefield, I was in the field hospital when I got an urgent call from Shawn. He hadn't heard the news yet, but he said he felt as if something bad had happened. He felt it all the way across the world." Riley sighed and wiped at his eyes. "It'll be like laying a piece of myself to rest."

"Did you feel it"—I paused—"Sunday morning, did you know something was wrong?" It seemed that twin connection would be extra strong if one of the twins had died.

Riley stopped and thought about it. "You know, I don't think I did. I was sleeping, so that might be it or maybe it was just because we were no longer as close." His face dropped along with his shoulders.

It wasn't a huge, outward show of emotion, but it appeared genuine. The man had seen war. It was more than likely that he'd learned to keep his emotions in check as part of his military training.

He stared at the box of flowers. "I'm not sure what to do with all these."

"You could take them to the retirement home on Butternut Crest. I'm sure they'd love to have some flowers."

Riley seemed to consider the suggestion. "Good idea."

We turned and walked back to gather up more flowers. "If you don't mind me asking—well—" I rarely found it hard to ask what was on my mind, but, suddenly, it felt cruel bringing up Riley's relationship with Amanda.

He stopped and looked at me. "You've heard that Amanda and I were together before I went to war."

I felt my face warm with shame. But since he'd brought it up, I carried on. "I heard that you were expecting to marry Amanda after high school."

We scooped up more flowers.

"That was my plan. Then I decided to join the military. It was something I dreamed about as a kid, only the reality of war was very different once I got there. I went through three operations and four skin grafts. I had an amazing medical team."

"Thank goodness for that."

"I left the army thinking I'd come home to Amanda waiting for me with wedding bells in her eyes. We'd written many times, and she never once mentioned that she'd been dating Shawn. He never brought it up either."

"Maybe they didn't want to get inside your head or mess with your emotions while you were doing such an important, dangerous job overseas," I suggested. My heartstrings were being pulled big time, and I felt guilty even thinking Riley could have killed them.

"That's what they told me, of course. Didn't make it much

easier because I had to absorb the full impact of their betrayal once I got home to recover."

His use of the word *betrayal* snapped my radar to attention. Was I writing him off too fast?

"You still loved Amanda," I said as a statement and not a question.

We carried the last armfuls of flowers to the box. The retirement home was going to be lit up with blooms this afternoon.

Riley reached into the box and pulled out a small teddy bear that was attached to a bouquet. "I bought Amanda one just like this for Valentine's Day, sophomore year. She still has it, I think. And to answer your question, yes, I still loved her. But she made it clear she was with Shawn for the duration." Riley shook his head. "My brother sometimes worked hard to be void of charm. We might have looked identical, but we had little else in common."

"Except loving Amanda," I said.

"Yes, except that. I didn't kill them," he stated without warning.

I looked at him.

"I know you're with Detective Jackson and that you write a lot of newspaper articles about murder, but it wasn't me. What they did broke my spirit for a long time, but I've rebounded. First thing I did was free myself from the family business." He glanced around. "This mill. It was never going to be my future. I love landscaping. I love what I do. I'm feeling alone right now, but I've got friends, coworkers who'll help me get through this." He looked across the yard. "Just stack them there,

Tucker. The rental place will pick them up this afternoon. Tucker is a good buddy. We used to play on the soccer team."

"Did you know that Tucker Carmichael kept a gun in his glove box?" It was an abrupt transition, but the mention of his friendship with Tucker had reminded me about the gun.

Riley rubbed his brow absently. "I know he likes to shoot. He's a good shot, too. I once saw him take out a snake from a good fifteen feet away. The glove box?" he asked to make sure.

"Yes, he kept it there for emergencies...like snakes."

Riley looked over at Tucker. He was working hard, folding up the chairs and setting them in neat stacks. "I don't think he ever showed it to me." Riley looked at me. "I haven't touched a gun since I left the service. Just haven't had the urge to pick one up, and while I knew Tucker had a gun, I never noticed or asked where he kept it."

Riley looked down at the big box of flowers and sighed. "I guess I'll drive these over to the retirement home. Thanks for the suggestion. I think it'll help my mood."

"Take care of yourself," I said.

My phone rang before I reached the Jeep. It was Jackson. "Hey, how's it going?"

"Not great," Jackson said. "There was a body in a backyard pond, but I think we'll be zeroing in on the killer soon. They left behind some clear footprints. How was the memorial?"

"It was nice. A lot of people came, but no one looked suspicious or fidgety. I found out something interesting." I looked toward the farmyard. Riley was loading the box of flowers into the back of his truck. "Did you know Riley and Amanda had a romantic past?"

"He mentioned that they dated in high school."

"Well, Riley tried to get Amanda to take him back—or at least, that is the interpretation of the scene Danielle, one of the mill staff, saw on Saturday. Amanda turned him down. I just spoke with Riley, and he admits he still loved her. He also insists he didn't kill them."

"And now is when you tell me he sounded genuine about it, and I remind you that there are some pretty good actors out there. Sorry, that sounded snarky."

"It sure as heck did," I said.

"Too many murders. Why do so many people kill each other? I plan to talk to Riley later today."

"All right. I think I'm going to stick around here at the mill for a bit. Tucker is cleaning up, and I want to see how he's doing. I guess I haven't mentioned this yet, but Raine broke up with him last night. She was tired of him never having money. She's been paying for everything."

"There could be an entire soap opera written about Raine's life," Jackson quipped.

"Well, not everyone is lucky enough to settle down with Mr. Snark. You know, being drop-dead gorgeous will only get you so far in life."

"Jeez, I get it. I'm being miserable. But you think I'm drop-dead gorgeous?" he asked.

"Yes, but that wasn't the part you were supposed to make note of. I was thinking—we should have a nice candlelit dinner after you finish these cases. We can celebrate and rekindle a little romance. Feels like that's been lacking—"

"Be right there," Jackson called abruptly to someone. "Hey, Bluebird, gotta go. I'll see you later." He hung up.

I stared at the phone in my hand. "Well, that went well."

Tucker was almost finished with the chairs. I decided to talk to him a little more. I wasn't taking anyone off the list yet, and that was more aggravating than encouraging—even more so after that last phone call with Jackson.

CHAPTER 31

Tucker had finished piling the chairs, and he was walking around picking up some of the litter left behind by the mourners. He turned quickly at the sound of my footsteps, placed his hand against his chest and smiled. "Guess I'm a little jumpy after what happened here," he said with a chuckle. He shoved a few napkins in the trash bag he was holding and chuckled again. "Guess old habits really do die hard. I've been taking care of this place for three years." His expression saddened. "Can't believe I won't be working here anymore. The mill kind of grew on me."

The afternoon sun had broken through the clouds, and sunlight poured through the surrounding trees and their fiery fall foliage. The farmhouse looked as if it belonged in a bucolic oil painting, and the mill sat looking stoic and historical and worthy of admiration. The property felt picturesque and serene. It was hard to believe two people had been shot to death here just days before.

"How are you doing?" I asked. "I mean other than—you know—the breakup with Raine? Any job prospects?"

Tucker shook his head dejectedly. "I'm searching, but I already know it's going to be tough. I talked to Riley earlier when we were setting up the chairs. I was hoping he needed someone at his landscaping company. He said they were kind of slow right now, what with winter coming, but he was sure he could find a spot for me in spring."

I smiled. "Well, that's something."

"Yeah, except I've still got to make it through the rest of fall and winter." He gave himself a little shake. "Enough feeling sorry for yourself, Tucker," he chuckled. "What did you think about the memorial? I thought Riley did a good job organizing it. I noticed you were helping him with the flowers. That was kind of you. You had a nice chat, too. How was he doing?"

"He's holding up pretty well...considering." I saw my opportunity and hoped it wouldn't be too clumsy or awkward. "Tucker, this might sound like an off-the-wall question, but do you think Riley knew about the gun you kept in your glove box?"

Tucker's fuzzy brows bunched up in confusion, then his face smoothed in comprehension. "You don't think—no, he wouldn't kill his own brother—would he? Then again, they never really got along, and Shawn stole Amanda away from Riley. If you'd seen Riley and Amanda in high school—they were so smitten with each other. I'm not sure I'd forgive my brother if he stole my girl. And while I was away at war, no less."

I'd started a small wildfire with my spark, but I hadn't

expected him to take off like that. "I'm sure he was distraught, but it's been many years," I said to remind him this was all just conjecture.

"Right, yes, of course. Time heals all wounds, as they say. But to answer your question—yes, Riley knew I had a gun in my truck." Tucker smiled coyly. "I probably brag too much about my shooting skills. When I was a kid, I won several trophies for target shooting. I'm sure I showed it to him. He knew I killed a few venomous snakes on the property. Probably stupid to brag to an ex-soldier about my shooting expertise," he added. "I couldn't enlist because of a heart murmur."

I hadn't expected his answer, and it was certainly adding some twists and turns to my investigation. Had Riley lied to me? If so, that would put him at the top of the suspect list. And if his heartbreak and sense of betrayal had lasted all these years—which, according to Danielle's story, it had—then Riley had motive.

"Well, I should get going," I said. I needed to head over to the retirement home. With any luck, I'd meet up with Riley. Then I could ask him a few more questions.

I walked toward the Jeep and noticed an elderly man with a cane walking slowly toward the cider mill. "Am I too late?" he asked in a creaky voice. He was breathing hard, and his hands shook slightly as he jammed the cane on the ground and leaned on it. "I overslept. I was hoping to make it to the memorial."

"I'm sorry to say you missed it. It was a very nice memorial, though. Are you a friend or—"

"Neighbor. Name's Mike. I live with my daughter, Megan. She and Sam had to go to work, but I'd planned on attending.

It's my crazy old man sleep pattern," he said with a hoarse chuckle. "I'm up at the crack of dawn, wide awake, and then noon rolls around and I'm out cold."

"I do that same thing during summer when the sun starts coming up too early. I'm up with the sun, and by lunchtime, I'm dreaming about a nap." I was anxious to find Riley at the retirement home, but Mike was so sweet, and he'd made it all the way to the mill on a cane and two unsteady legs. Something occurred to me as we were talking. "Do you always get up at the crack of dawn?"

"Most days, yes. This blasted cold air—" He pulled a linen handkerchief out of his trouser pocket and wiped his nose.

"Were you up early on Sunday, the day of the murders?" I asked.

"Sure was. I'm one of those old fossils who reads the Sunday paper from cover to cover every Sunday morning with a cup of coffee and a marmalade toast at my side. The paperboy brings the paper early, around five. It was already on the porch when I woke up."

"I don't suppose you saw anything that morning? Anything that might be important?"

His grin was as kind as his demeanor. "Do you know you're the first person to ask me that? The police came to the door, and they spoke with Megan and Sam, but no one asked me if I'd seen anything." He shrugged. "I guess when you get to my age, no one wants to hear anything from you. But I saw something. It was that produce man. The crates in the back of his truck always clatter like wooden teeth." He clacked his teeth together a few times. "He pulled into the mill. I thought it was awfully early, but I knew they were expecting a lot of visitors.

There's so much dust and noise when they open the mill for the weekend."

"What time did you see him?"

"Gosh." He unfolded his handkerchief and folded it again before putting it back in his pocket. "I was on the third page. There was an interesting article about bird migration. I glanced up at the clock on the kitchen wall when his truck rattled past. It was half-past seven. But the funny thing about it was he raced back by just ten minutes later. Tore off like his hair was on fire."

I stood there for a second, taking in the information he was happily handing out and processing it with shock. All this time, this man had huge information, and no one had thought to ask him if he'd seen anything the day of the murder. And boy, had he seen something. Jackson had been leaning toward Jonah as the key suspect right from the start. I supposed that was his detective's instinct kicking in.

"Mike, if you don't mind, I'm going to tell Detective Jackson about what you saw. He'll probably want to ask you a few questions."

"Sure, sure," he said. "Don't have much planned today." He chuckled. "I like to watch the four o'clock news, though. The anchors on the five o'clock news are unbearable. They are constantly laughing and joking as if they're on a talk show and not up there delivering the important news of the day."

I nodded. "Yes, 'Joe and Trish at Five.' I agree. Mike, can I give you a lift back home? My Jeep is closer than your house."

"Oh, no, I need the exercise."

"All right. Thanks so much for stopping to talk to me," I said. "I'm sorry you missed the memorial."

"And thank you for asking me what I saw that morning. It's nice to know I'm not invisible to everyone."

"Yes, I'm sorry that happened. It's been delightful talking to you. Enjoy the rest of your day."

I hurried to my Jeep and sent Jackson a quick text. "I've got new information. Call me when you get this."

CHAPTER 32

I'd really hoped to hear from Jackson before I reached Jonah's produce stand, but he must have been too busy to get back to me. I was doubly disappointed I hadn't heard from Jackson when I saw that Jonah was working the produce stand alone. I considered for a moment not getting out of the Jeep, but I badly wanted to get the Griswold murder solved. After all, I had a story to write.

Jonah was explaining to a woman how to bake the purple sweet potatoes she was holding. I browsed the vegetables while they talked. There was a stand of bagged candy near the apples. I picked up a bag of chocolate covered peanuts to buy. They were Jackson's favorite. They'd make a nice dessert for the romantic dinner I'd been planning.

The woman paid for her purple potatoes and left the stand. It was just me and Jonah and my bag of chocolate peanuts. He seemed to recognize me but pretended not to.

"Just the peanuts?" he asked as he circled around to his cash register.

"Uh, yes, just the peanuts." I was feeling nervous about this endeavor, but I couldn't chicken out now. I needed to put on my big girl journalist pants and ask the important questions, no matter what the consequences. Of course, I'd already calculated that it would take him a few seconds to get back around the cash register, which would give me and my long, fast legs a head start to the Jeep. Still, it took me longer than usual to work up my courage. Jonah was a rather intimidating looking man.

"I was at the memorial for Amanda and Shawn Griswold." It seemed like the easiest way to bring up the murders.

Jonah grunted in response.

"I guess you didn't get a chance to go," I said. "It was well-attended, and many people had nice things to say about them."

Jonah lifted his face and stared plainly at me as he took the cash from my hand.

"You know, I wonder if you almost came face-to-face with the killer on Sunday morning. I heard you were at the mill around half-past seven."

We were under the shade of the produce stand, but I could see some color drain from his face. "Nope," was all he said.

"Oh, that's interesting. Must have been someone else driving your produce truck." I added a shocked gasp. "My goodness, was it your wife? She probably just missed running into the killer. Although, the people who saw your truck were sure they saw you behind the wheel." I shrugged as if it was no big deal that he was at the mill around the time of the murders. "Just heard it in conversation at the memorial."

"You're with Detective Jackson, aren't you?" So, he did recognize me. I thought as much.

"Why, yes, I am. But he wasn't at the memorial this afternoon."

"Well, I don't have anything else to say about the matter."

"That's fine. I'm sure you've already explained to Detective Jackson why you were at the mill Sunday morning."

Jonah started fidgeting with a display of home baked cookies at the counter. As he did so, two fell on the floor in front of the register.

I stooped down and picked them up. "Guess it's good these were wrapped in cellophane." I was keeping up an airy tone and cheery smile. Jonah, on the other hand, looked nervous. I was sure I detected a slight twitch in his eye as he returned the cookies to the display.

"I didn't kill them" he said suddenly. He looked up at me. "They were—they were already dead. I didn't say anything cuz Detective Jackson was never going to believe me, but maybe you can tell him for me."

I nodded as I absorbed the stunning confession. "I could do that. Why were you there? I saw Shawn and you arguing on Saturday, outside the mill. I heard him fire you. Why did you go back on Sunday?" I was feeling strangely at ease considering this conversation had gone in a completely different direction than I anticipated. But now, it seemed, I wasn't looking at a killer. Just a man who knew the Griswolds had been shot but didn't dare speak up for fear he'd be blamed.

Jonah shook his head. "It was stupid, but I went back to try and talk Griswold into rehiring me. After he fired me, I was relieved that I wouldn't be working with him anymore. All he ever did was complain, and he was always late paying his invoices, too. Still, Susan asked me to try and get the account back because the mill is our main client in the fall. Plus, we're getting a shipment of apples in this week, and without the mill, we're going to end up with a surplus, and we'll have to absorb the cost on our own."

"What happened once you got to the mill?"

He paused. I sensed that the whole scene had freaked him out. He'd managed to act cool as a cucumber when Jackson spoke to him, but in reality, he was still recovering from the shock of it. "I walked to the mill. I noticed the door was slightly ajar. I called inside, but there was no answer, so I headed to the house. I knocked on the kitchen door, expecting Annie or Amanda to be in the kitchen getting pies ready for the day's event. Again, no answer. So, I walked around to the kitchen window and peered inside. I was just tall enough to see the kitchen floor near the worktable. That's when I saw Amanda on the floor. I saw the blood and she looked—" He took a deep breath. "In my early twenties, my best friend shot himself. I was the one who found him in his garage. I know what death looks like. I knew Amanda was dead. I ran to the mill hoping to find Shawn, all the while wondering if he'd shot his own wife. That was when I saw Shawn, face down in the pomace." He leaned back against the table behind the register. It seemed to have taken all his energy to tell his story. "I panicked and raced back to my truck and left. It wasn't me. I know I should have called the police right then, but I was sure they'd haul me in for murder."

I hated to admit it, but I believed his story. "Did you know about Tucker's gun?"

"Tucker's gun? Not sure what you're talking about. I know the guy was into guns and shooting practice. He asked me once or twice if I ever did any shooting. I told him I only had a gun for protection."

"So, you don't know where he keeps the gun?" I asked.

"Nope, I never talked to the guy much. Mostly, he just waved me onto the property, told me where to park and occasionally helped unload crates."

"You never went up to the trail," I said.

"I did but only for a few minutes to drink my coffee and work up the courage to go beg Griswold to hire me back."

My phone rang in my pocket. I was sure it was Jackson, and Jonah seemed to sense it, too.

"I'll let Detective Jackson know what you told me. I'm sure he'll want to take you in for questions, but just tell him the truth. The real killer will be caught soon."

Jonah nodded. "Yeah, sure hope so."

I walked away with my bag of peanuts and my phone. "Hey, where are you?"

Jackson grunted in frustration. "I'm at the precinct processing this arrest. We've got a signed confession, so it shouldn't take too long. What have you heard?"

I got in my Jeep. Jonah was carrying a crate of potatoes out to his truck. He glanced back a few times toward the Jeep. "Jonah Dowd was at the mill on Sunday morning about half-past seven. I spoke to an eyewitness, which is another story in itself. Jonah went to the mill to beg Shawn to rehire him as the mill produce man. But when he got there, he came upon the grisly scenes in the house and the mill. He says the Griswolds were already dead. He panicked, and he ran. I get the sense he's telling the truth."

"Uh-huh," Jackson said wryly.

"See, that's why he didn't call the police. He was sure no one would believe him."

"Wait. Are you there with him now? Are you alone—"

"Calm down, Detective Jackson, I'm in my Jeep, and my reporter's intuition is telling me Jonah is innocent. But I'll let you decide that. He told me, hoping I'd relay it to you and soften the impact. Has it worked?"

"Not really. He lied when I spoke to him, and that never looks good. However, it also does make sense that he didn't want to speak up and find himself arrested for murder. I'll get over to talk to him just as soon as I'm done here. Where are you off to? Back home?"

"Soon but not yet. There are a couple other rocks I need to overturn before my investigation is over. I'll see you later."

"Don't do anything dangerous," he blurted before I could hang up.

CHAPTER 33

I'd gotten badly sidetracked from my original plan to catch Riley at the retirement home. My side trip to Jonah's produce stand had been worth the detour. So much was peeling open on the case, I sensed I was getting closer to the endgame. I drove quickly along Butternut Crest. The Hickory Flats Retirement Home was a set of blue buildings a mile or so off the highway. I was in luck. Riley was just exiting the building. His gait was slow and hindered by his bad leg, but he was smiling as he walked to his car.

I pulled into the lot and caught up to him as he opened his car door. "Hello, Riley."

He turned back to see who'd called him and looked surprised to see me. Which was...not surprising. "Yes? Miss Taylor. What are you doing here?"

"I thought I could help distribute the flowers, but I see you've already finished." I wasn't convinced he was buying my excuse.

"Uh, yes, there were enough flowers for a bouquet in each room and a few in the communal dining area. Thank you for the suggestion. You didn't need to make the trip out here," he said with an edge of skepticism. "Is there something else you'd like from me?"

"All right, you got me. I wasn't out here to help. Although I'm glad my suggestion helped."

Riley glanced back at the building. "Yes, they were very excited, and it helped lighten my dark mood. Why *did* you drive all the way out here?"

After confronting Jonah, I found I was still wearing those big girl journalist pants. "I spoke with Tucker after we talked. He said you knew about the gun in his glove box."

"If he showed it to me, I certainly don't remember." He shut the door on his car, crossed his arms and stood up straighter. "Are you accusing me of something? Because it seems as if that's what's going on here." He was more defensive and, admittedly, a little scarier than Jonah. Had I finally cornered the killer? It was in bad taste for me to think it, but I was sure I could outrun him with his bad leg.

"I'm not accusing you. I'm just trying to get the story straight."

Riley grinned, but it wasn't a kind grin. "I see. You're a reporter trying to find the most scandalous ending to my brother and sister-in-law's murders. I loved them both. I didn't always show it to Shawn, but he knew. And he loved me. I was hurt that Amanda and Shawn got together behind my back, but after what I'd gone through on the battlefield, I could never take another life—not ever again." His voice grew frail and shaky. "You don't recover from that easily—killing another human." His pensive expression reminded me of Edward whenever he was drawn off to a distant sad moment.

"I'm sorry," I said. "It seems I've brought up a lot of memories you'd prefer not to relive. It's just that Tucker told me you knew about the gun in his truck."

Riley looked directly at me. "Clearly, one of us isn't telling the truth. If he had pointed it out to me, I wasn't paying attention."

"I wonder why Tucker would lie about it?" I asked. Like with Jonah, my intuition was telling me Riley was innocent. "Do you think he was trying to implicate you in the murders?"

"I have no idea." Riley blew out an aggravated puff of air. "It's why I kept clear of that whole darn mill business. It was always a big soap opera. Shawn was always on the verge of firing someone for this or that. Frankly, I'm almost surprised this didn't happen sooner. He angered a lot of people. I hate to say this about my own brother, especially now, but he seemed to enjoy making people miserable. He loved the power that came with being the boss, being able to end someone's livelihood with a snap of his fingers. He had a preprinted notepad with official employment termination notices. He'd fire the person first, verbally, and then make sure he covered his legal bases by sending them an official notice. It was like a double shot of espresso for him."

A breeze pushed through the lot and a hurricane of leaves followed. It wouldn't be long before all the deciduous trees along the highway were down to bare branches.

Something Riley said triggered a memory. "Notices," I said. "He sent out notices."

"That's right. Like I said—he had a whole pad of them to

tear off when needed. I told him one day he'd run out of people to hire, but like I said, he seemed to enjoy giving people the axe."

"I saw a sticky note on his desk." I smiled coyly. "Might have been snooping around. The sticky note said 'Write three notices.' Do you think he was talking about employment termination notices?"

"Not sure what other notices he'd be writing," Riley said.

"But why three?" I asked. "I was at the mill on Saturday. I witnessed him firing Jonah. And you're right. He did seem to take a certain amount of joy in it. Hours later he was firing Annie for burning the pies. But who was number three?"

Riley rubbed his chin. "Not sure. He texted me after he fired Jonah. Not sure why but he always filled me in on the mill business. I don't know who else was on the firing list. Boy, he really was on a roll that day. There are only a few part-time people he hires seasonally to run the kiosks at special events. Maybe one of them got fired. Tucker was with them for three years. He occasionally messed up, and Shawn would yell at him and threaten to fire him, but my brother knew that Tucker worked hard, and he knows that mill inside and out. Frankly, Shawn didn't like to get his hands dirty much. He preferred to give Tucker the hard work."

"Well, I won't keep you," I said. "I know this has been a trying few days for you."

Riley smiled weakly. "So, you're not going to make a citizen's arrest?"

"Not today, no."

Riley opened his car door again. "By the way, where *is*

Detective Jackson? I'm anxious for him to make an arrest and bring their killer to justice."

"Unfortunately, he got called away on another case, but I expect him to be back full-time on this one before the end of the day."

"Let him know to contact me as soon as he makes an arrest," Riley said.

"I will. Take care."

I headed to the Jeep. It was time to give Tucker a more thorough consideration. If he'd been the third person Shawn fired, then his motive just got a whole lot stronger.

CHAPTER 34

A brisk, persistent breeze had kicked up, and it seemed to be staying for the duration of the afternoon. I drove to Tucker's house. I needed to know if he'd been fired by Shawn. I wasn't sure if I'd get an honest answer or not, but he'd been using his desperate need for that job to show why he couldn't possibly be the killer. Then there was the gun in the glove box issue. It was one man's word against the other, but I was leaning toward Riley being the one telling the truth. After I asked Tucker about it, he went off on a long tangent about Riley and his heartbreak. Was he trying to push Riley into the center of the investigation?

I was surprised when I pulled into Tucker's neighborhood. He was washing a blue sedan. His truck was parked out on the street. I parked and got out of the Jeep. Tucker was facing the car, wiping it down with a sudsy sponge. The little neighbor dog, Tiger, came bounding across the driveway as I reached it. He barked sharply at me, alerting Tucker that he had a visitor.

"Tiger, that's enough," Tucker said sharply, and the dog stopped barking and trotted over to Tucker's porch steps.

Tucker wrung out the sponge. "Sunni, I didn't expect to see you here." His eyes rounded. "Have you spoken to Raine?" he asked hopefully. This whole investigation would have been a lot easier if Raine's relationship hadn't been tangled up in it. First, I was working to clear Tucker's name so that Raine wouldn't be heartbroken. Then, Raine herself decided the relationship was a dead end. Now I was back trying to figure out if Tucker was the killer, and in the meantime, he was the one dealing with the heartbreak. It made him a much more sympathetic suspect. Still, he was a suspect. If he did turn out to be the killer, at least Raine's emotional ties had already been severed.

"I haven't spoken to her. I'm sorry. I came here to ask you something."

He lifted the sponge and pointed to the car. "Hope you don't mind if I keep washing my car. I don't want to get water spots."

"No, please, go ahead." I paused to replay something he said. "Wait, so this is your car?" I glanced pointedly at the truck parked on the street.

"It stays mostly in the garage. I don't take it out much. An old friend needed the cash, so I gave him five hundred dollars for it. Only use it when the truck isn't working."

Or when you want to leave the house quietly, I thought to myself. I'd all but cleared Tucker from the suspect list because the neighbors hadn't heard his truck leave before nine, long past the murder hour. But all this time, he had a second car, one that was probably much quieter than the truck. I still needed a motive.

"Tucker, when I was in Shawn's office, that day when we were both trespassing"—I added a smile to keep him off guard—"I saw a note Shawn had written, apparently to himself. It said he needed to write three notices. I assume those were employment termination notices."

He began rubbing the sponge much more vigorously. I followed him to the back of the car.

"I wouldn't know anything about that." Tucker said. He shoved the sponge into the bucket of soapy water. It dripped heavily as he returned the sponge to the car.

"Riley told me his brother took pleasure in firing people, and he even had a special pad that he used to give people official termination notices."

"Uh-huh, well, Riley would know more about that than me. My job was on the property and in the mill." He paused. "You should be talking to Riley, not me," he said sharply.

"I did talk to Riley. He said he didn't know about your gun in the glove box."

He swept the sponge over the car. Water sprayed my shoes. It seemed intentional. I backed up a few steps just in case. My interviewee was becoming irritated with the questioning. I glanced toward the house. Tucker's work boots were sitting next to the door, and the dog was wagging his tail as he licked the boots. Dogs and their love of all things gross, I thought with an inner smile.

"Riley probably just forgot," Tucker said tersely. "Either that or he's trying to prove his innocence. He knew about the gun, and he obviously decided to use my gun, so I'd be framed for the murders he committed. Riley has motive. I don't," he said succinctly. He was no longer playing at suggesting Riley did it. He was outright accusing him.

"Unless you were the third termination notice," I said grimly.

Tucker's shoulders tensed as I said it, but he continued to focus on the car. He glanced up long enough to shout at the dog. "Tiger, go home. Leave those boots alone." He swept the sponge over the top of the car and accidentally made eye contact with me.

"I know Shawn was firing a lot of people on Saturday. Did he fire you as well?"

"That's nonsense." Tucker threw the sponge into the bucket. Water splashed over the side. I stepped instinctively back as he picked up the hose. A dousing with cold hose water didn't sound the least bit inviting on such a brisk afternoon.

"Is it?" I asked.

He responded by turning on the hose full blast. The noise of the water hitting the car drowned out our conversation. Tucker pretended to be fully absorbed in his task. In the meantime, the small dog had ignored Tucker's command to go home because he was still licking the work boots. His tongue lapped at the edges of the soles. What could possibly be so delicious on a pair of boots? The second the question flashed through my head, I had an answer, and it sent a shot of adrenaline through me.

Tucker's neighbor, Lisa Ingersol, had perfect timing. She stepped out onto her porch and called for Tiger. The dog didn't hear her over the roar of the hose.

I waved to her. "I'll get him," I said. I ran to Tucker's front porch and bound up the steps. That was all Tiger needed to pull his attention from the boot. He raced down the steps and toward his own yard.

Tucker was still focused on washing his car, but he seemed far more tense than when the conversation started. I quickly picked up a work boot and turned it so I could see the sole. Like most work boots, it was heavy with a thick tread. Only most work boots didn't have cinnamon sugar tucked between the treads. I wiped my finger along one crevice to pull the sugar out. I took a whiff. It was faint, but I could smell the cinnamon. The footprint in the spilled cinnamon sugar and the granules on the way to the door—they were tracked there by Tucker Carmichael.

I was so stunned by my find that I hadn't noticed the hose turned off until the steps behind me creaked. I spun around. Tucker looked in confusion at his boot.

I smiled and placed it back down next to its mate. "I've been wanting to buy a new pair of boots for when I work outside in the barn. Are these comfortable?" I couldn't hide the tremble in my voice. I was standing on a small porch sandwiched between a killer and his very solid front door. The killer was pretty solid, too.

An evil expression took over his face. "What exactly do you want? You sure are nosy."

"I'm a reporter, remember? But you're right. I'm being far too nosy. I'll just be off. Maybe I'll even give Raine a call and see if I can bring her around. I hate to see your relationship end." Nothing in my tone sounded genuine, but my intuition, the one that was as helpful as it was a catalyst for trouble, had kicked in. Jackson had warned me to stay out of danger, and for once, I wished I'd listened to the man.

Tucker took another step up. I backed up, but I wouldn't be able to go much farther due to the inconvenient house behind me. I glanced toward the wet car. "Water spots," I said abruptly. "You need to dry your car before it gets water spots. I could help. Do you have an extra rag?" I forced a smile.

"The paint on that car is so faded, it doesn't matter. Let's you and I go inside for a chat, eh?" His tone sounded ominous and nothing like his usual one. He stepped up to the porch. I considered trying to push past him, but he was big and sturdy, and I had no room for a running start. My only hope was that I could talk my way out of this whole predicament.

"Right. Let's go in for that chat," I said. I considered a scenario where he reached for the door and I slipped past and ran for the Jeep.

That small glimmer of hope was dashed when he motioned to the doorknob. "It's open," he said. "After you." The grin that appeared next did not give me much hope that I'd be able to talk my way out of this. Next time, I'd listen to Jackson.

CHAPTER 35

I kept walking through the small, untidy house because Tucker followed close at my heels. "Right through to the kitchen," Tucker said harshly.

We reached his tiny kitchen. There was a pot with dried spaghetti sauce on the stove. The sink was filled with dirty dishes. I startled when Tucker yanked out a kitchen chair. It stuttered across the floor. "Sit," he ordered.

I sat down. "Look, I'm not sure what has you so upset. Maybe you're right. I should be talking to Riley. He—"

"Enough. Just stop talking." He paced a short path in front of me. "I need to think."

"Think about what?" I asked meekly but with a forced smile.

He stopped in front of me and glowered down. "About how I'm going to get rid of you for good."

"You could just let me walk through that door, and I promise you'll never see me again," I suggested hopefully.

"You sure do talk a lot."

"I could call Raine. Maybe we could set up a little meeting, and you two could get back together." I was throwing it all out there, but Tucker seemed determined to rid himself of the pesky journalist once and for all. I might as well at least get a confession for all my troubles. "So, Shawn did fire you. That was your motive," I added.

Tucker scrubbed his fingers through his hair, and he started pacing again. "I worked for that man for three years. Did everything. All the hard work—that fell on me. You should have seen his hands—like the soft skin on a newborn." Tucker stopped in front of me and showed me the palms of his hands. "Look at those calluses and blisters. All to keep his mill running."

I'd found a new angle to delay my possible murder. It was time to pull out the empathy wild card and hope it worked. "Not fair at all. When Raine and I were there, I saw how hard you worked. There was no way that place could run without you."

"Darn right, it couldn't. And I had to put up with his constant criticism. Nothing I did was ever good enough. Never a 'thanks' or a 'nice work, Tucker.' And Amanda was no better. She never spoke up or told Shawn he was being too harsh." His posture had softened, which gave me some hope.

I tried to relax myself, but I really had to work at it. "What caused him to fire you?"

Tucker rubbed his face as he paced. "It was something stupid. I left the water running in the mill, and there was a puddle of water under the apple press."

"That's it?" I asked. I didn't have to fake the incredulous

tone. It was a ridiculous reason to fire someone. Shawn really was a tyrant.

"That's all. I hurried to mop it up, and he stood back and watched with that smug grin. I got the mess cleaned up and was carrying out the mop. That's when he said it. 'You're fired.' Just like that."

"Totally unfair." A brilliant idea popped into my head that was really going to add gloss to my empathy ploy. "You know what? I'll write your story in the paper and let people know what a terrible boss Shawn Griswold was and what a stellar employee you were. I'm certain you'll get all kinds of offers of employment." I was laying it on thick, and for a second, it seemed he was buying it.

He paced back and forth a few times as if he was considering my offer. Then he stopped and shook his head. "Sorry, you won't be writing that story. Or any other stories," he said grimly.

There was a knock on the door. He stiffened, and his eyes nearly bulged from his face. "Did you tell that detective you were here? Stay put and not a word." He went to a kitchen drawer, opened it and pulled out a handgun.

My heartbeat sped up and adrenaline filled my veins. There was another knock. It was soft enough that I knew it wasn't Jackson. I was relieved. I feared Jackson would walk into an ambush.

The door opened, and Tucker readied his gun. I'd heard far too many times this week about what a good shot he was.

"Tucker?" An all-too-familiar voice floated into the house. "It's me, Raine. I thought we could talk."

Tucker shot me a quelling glance, shoved his gun into the

waistband of his pants and pulled his shirt down over it. "Stay put or she's dead," he muttered through a tight jaw.

Raine pushed the door open wider. "Oh, there you are. I saw that your car was wet, so I figured you'd gone inside to get some rags." Raine hadn't seen me sitting in the kitchen yet.

"That's right. I'm in the middle of washing the car. Maybe we could meet at the coffee shop, say in an hour," Tucker suggested pleasantly. Apparently, it was only going to take an hour to kill me and make me disappear.

Tucker was blocking the room with his wide physique, but that didn't stop Raine from stepping farther inside. "I could help with the car. I was thinking maybe I've made a mistake," she said sweetly. (She had definitely not made a mistake.)

"I'm so happy to hear that, but you don't have to help—"

"Sunni?" Raine said suddenly. She leaned to get a better look past Tucker. "Sunni, what are you doing here?"

I forced a smile. I needed to get my friend to leave without too many questions. I didn't want her to get dragged into this mess. "Still trying to get to the bottom of the Griswold murder. Tucker has some great insight into all the people Shawn angered in the past few years. I've got a whole list of names to look at."

Tucker nodded. "That's right, and to be honest, Raine, I was asking her how I might win you back."

Raine moved closer to me. I'd stayed put on the chair just like Tucker asked. I wasn't going to do anything to throw things out of whack. I was sure Tucker wouldn't think twice about killing both of us.

Raine smiled lightly. "So, you two are conspiring, eh?" she asked with a laugh. Her gaze landed on me, and she stared at me for a long moment, then turned. "I guess we could meet at the coffee shop in an hour," Raine said. She walked out the door. I practically collapsed in relief. The last thing I wanted was for Raine to get hurt.

Tucker came back to the kitchen. "Well done." He pulled out his gun. "I'm almost sorry I have to kill you."

The sound of breaking glass was followed by a groan. Tucker's eyes rolled up in his head, and he crumpled to the floor. My best friend was standing behind him holding the broken half of a lamp. "Jerk," she said. "And I almost took him back."

I jumped up, grabbed her hand and the two of us ran out to the street. We hid behind the Jeep as I called the police. They were on their way. Raine and I hugged.

"You saved my life," I said, half sobbing.

"I guess I kind of did. I can't believe I was going to take that jerk back. Boy, I'm terrible at picking men."

I smiled up at her. "I guess you kind of are." We both laughed. "How did you know something was up?" I asked.

Raine tapped the side of her head. "Sixth sense, remember?"

I hugged her again. "I love you and your sixth sense." My phone rang. I was still jittery with adrenaline, so I startled at the sound of it. It was Jackson.

"Hey, Jax."

"I just heard something on dispatch. Where are you right now? Or do I want to know?"

"Raine and I are safely tucked behind the Jeep, and the killer is in his house, possibly still out cold or, at the very least, trying to shake the stars out of his head. Raine gave him a good smack with a lamp." I smiled at my friend. "She saved my life."

"I'm on my way," Jackson said. "And give Raine a hug for me."

"No problem." I put away my phone, and Raine and I hugged until the first patrol car arrived on the street.

CHAPTER 36

I set the electric candles down on the small table. There were far too many flammable things in the barn, including a wall of straw, to use real ones. These would do the trick. I'd covered a small card table with my best tablecloth, and I'd used the nicer dishes. A bouquet of cheery sunflowers was tucked into a glass vase in the center of the table. Emily's pecan pie was in the kitchen, waiting to be dolloped with whipped cream, but first Jackson and I were going to sit down to a dinner of pepper steak and baked potatoes.

The dogs weren't happy when I told them to stay in the house. Neither was the ghost. Of course, Edward was the reason I decided to move my romantic dinner plans out to the barn. There was little chance of alone time with a bored, arrogant spirit always hanging around. His arrogance had been in turbo mode because he'd felt all along that Tucker wasn't to be trusted.

If there was one thing Edward hated more than anything, it was Jackson and me trying to sneak some romance into our lives. Tonight, we were all alone. Cash snorted into his pile of hay just then, reminding me that we were *almost* alone.

I brushed off my dress. It was chilly outside, but my favorite white cardigan helped keep out the cold. I'd even clipped my hair up with two shiny barrettes I borrowed from Emily. She always had all the cute stuff. Me, not so much.

The back door opened and shut, and heavy footsteps came toward the barn. My breath caught in my chest as Jackson's broad shoulders filled the open doorway. He was wearing the black cowboy hat I bought him and a dark-gray button-down shirt.

"Ah, my dream date has arrived," I said.

Jackson's white smile flashed beneath the hat. He tipped the brim forward. "Little lady."

I laughed and hurried over to hug him. After the harrowing ending to my week, I was more than pleased to be having a quiet dinner at home. We kissed.

"Should we eat?" I asked once the kiss ended.

"Yes, I'm starved. And I'm not even going to check on Cash before I sit down."

I laughed. "Oh, go ahead."

He walked over to the stall, looked in on the horse and then hung his hat on a hook on the barn wall. We sat down at the table.

"And *I'm* not going to discuss the murder," I said.

"Sounds good."

I frowned. "You're supposed to say 'oh, go ahead.' Actually, you're right. This is supposed to be a romantic dinner. You can fill me in on all the details after dessert."

"Is dessert that pecan pie I saw on the counter?"

"Yes, and before you ask and hurt my feelings, yes, Emily baked it."

Jackson tamped down a smile as he unfolded his napkin and placed it on his lap. "This is nice. And no one hovering around making a nuisance of himself."

"That's why I planned the dinner out here. Plus, it's a beautiful fall night." I reached across to take hold of his hand. "I don't think I say this enough, but I'm so glad to have you in my life, Jax."

Jackson squeezed my hand. "I was just thinking the same thing about you, Bluebird."

Cash snorted loudly, and we both laughed.

"Yes, we are glad to have you in our lives, too, Cash," I said. "That horse is almost as needy as you-know-who in the house."

Jackson leaned over and kissed me once more. "The horse is great, but Sunni Taylor is the best partner a guy could ever have."

ABOUT THE AUTHOR

London Lovett is the author of the Firefly Junction, Port Danby, Scottie Ramone, Frostfall Island and Starfire Cozy Mystery series. She loves getting caught up in a good mystery and baking delicious new treats!

Subscribe to London's newsletter [londonlovett.com] to never miss an update.

You can also join London for fun discussions, giveaways and more in her **Secret Sleuths** Facebook group.

https://www.facebook.com/groups/londonlovettssecretsleuths/

Instagram @LondonLovettWrites
Facebook.com/LondonLovettWrites

Find all available books at LondonLovett.com

Made in United States
Troutdale, OR
08/19/2024